"My name is Charlaine, and
—Charlaine Harris, #1 *New York Times* bestselling author

"JoAnna Carl satisfies . . . your craving for a tasty whodunit."
—Cleo Coyle, *New York Times* bestselling author of
the Coffeehouse Mysteries

"Lee [Woodyard] sells chocolates and solves crimes with
panache and good humor."
—Carolyn Hart, *New York Times* bestselling author

"Lots of suspects, red herrings, and chocolate trivia."
—*Kirkus Reviews*

"A deft mix of truffles and trouble. Chocoholics—this book
is for you!"
—Laura Childs, *New York Times* bestselling author of
the Tea Shop Mysteries

"Delicious, fast-paced . . . more twists and turns than a
chocolate-covered pretzel!"
—Leslie Meier, *New York Times* bestselling author of
Candy Corn Murder

"A real page-turner, and I got chocolate on every one!"
—Tamar Myers, author of *Tea with Jam and Dread*

"Realistic characters, an engaging plot, and lots of local color
distinguish this superior cozy." —*Publishers Weekly*

"Deliciously cozy . . . richly entertaining, and has no
calories."
—Elaine Viets, national bestselling author of
the Dead-End Job Mysteries

Titles by JoAnna Carl

The Chocolate Cat Caper
The Chocolate Bear Burglary
The Chocolate Frog Frame-Up
The Chocolate Puppy Puzzle
The Chocolate Mouse Trap
The Chocolate Bridal Bash
The Chocolate Jewel Case
The Chocolate Snowman Murders
The Chocolate Cupid Killings
The Chocolate Pirate Plot
The Chocolate Castle Clue
The Chocolate Moose Motive
The Chocolate Book Bandit
The Chocolate Clown Corpse
The Chocolate Falcon Fraud
The Chocolate Bunny Brouhaha

Anthologies

Crime de Cocoa
Chocolate to Die For

The
Chocolate Bunny
Brouhaha

A Chocoholic Mystery

JoAnna Carl

BERKLEY PRIME CRIME
New York

BERKLEY PRIME CRIME
Published by Berkley
An imprint of Penguin Random House LLC
375 Hudson Street, New York, New York 10014

Copyright © 2016 by Eve Sandstrom

ISBN: 9780451473837

Berkley Prime Crime hardcover edition / November 2016
Berkley Prime Crime mass-market edition / November 2017

Printed in the United States of America
1 3 5 7 9 10 8 6 4 2

Cover art by Ben Perini

For Claire, Clay, and Eric.

Still the world's best grandkids.

Acknowledgments

I owe thanks to Buddy and Lisa Green who made a generous contribution to the Lawton–Fort Sill Arts for All campaign of Lawton, Oklahoma, in honor of their granddaughter Chayslee Brett Zimmerman, whose name appears in this book.

I also owe thanks to Jim Avance, a real-life detective, who advised me. If I got it wrong, it's my fault, not Jim's. Others who helped included my Michigan friends and neighbors Tracy Paquin, Susan McDermott, and Judy Hallisy. Plus the only architect to whom I'm related, my brother, Kim Kimbrell. My chocolate experts remain my daughter, Betsy Peters, and my pal Elizabeth Garber of Best Chocolate in Town, Indianapolis.

If I didn't have friends and relatives, I couldn't write a word.

Chapter 1

I always think of it as the afternoon of the Birdsong invasion.

It began with someone pounding on our back door and ringing the doorbell at the same time. TenHuis Chocolade seemed to be shaking with the sounds.

"What on earth?" I stood up and moved toward the door. "Whoever is out there must have three hands. It would take more than two to pound and punch that hard in unison."

I flipped the lock and swung the door open. "What's the matter?"

Bunny Birdsong rushed in, nearly knocking me flat. She's short, and I'm tall, and the two of us managed to get all mixed up. Arms and legs were every which way. I felt like a marionette with tangled strings.

Bunny was in a panic. "Quick! Quick! Close the door!"

She freed herself from our knot, whirled around, and slammed the door hard. She locked the dead bolt. Then she leaned back against the metal surface, panting. Her spiked blond hair was standing up straight, and her gray eyes were as big as poker chips.

"Thank God you were there to let me in, Lee! I was so frightened."

I stared. "What were you scared of, Bunny?"

"It was that man again! The one with the ski mask! He followed me down the alley!"

"Let me have a look," I said. I took Bunny by the arms and moved her aside. Then I unlocked the door and took hold of the handle.

But before I could turn it, Bunny had shoved herself in front of me again. "Don't open it, Lee! I'm sure he's dangerous!"

I beckoned to Dolly Jolly, who was sitting at one of our break room tables, staring at our performance. Dolly joined me at the door, and I spoke to Bunny, trying to keep my voice calm. "It's okay."

Dolly is more than six feet tall, husky, with brilliant and bushy red hair. I'm just a shade under six feet myself, not thin, with blond hair. Side by side, the two of us can make a big impression.

"Dolly and I are each as big as Goliath and as tough as Godzilla," I said. "We can scare anybody away."

"No, no!" Bunny sounded terrified.

I pushed the door open, and Dolly and I both peered around it. Then we stepped outside and looked up and down the alley. It was a crisp, sunny winter day in west Michigan, and there was no one near the back door of the TenHuis Chocolade shop.

Dolly yelled, "Nobody there!"

Dolly has one social flaw. She can't speak in a

normal tone of voice. Everything she says comes out in a shout.

"Bunny, I don't see a soul," I said.

Bunny still looked scared. She sank into a chair and covered her face with her hands. "I know I didn't imagine it."

"It was probably just some guy headed for the back door of the wine shop," I said. I tried to make my voice calm and soothing.

"I hope that's all it was," Bunny said. "I'm sorry. I didn't mean to cause any trouble."

She got to her feet, and her chair fell over behind her. She picked it up, knocking it into the edge of the table. The can of Diet Coke I'd been drinking teetered. I caught it. Then Bunny went toward the restroom, her head drooping and her feet dragging.

As soon as we heard the restroom exhaust fan start, Dolly spoke in the loud hiss that she used for a whisper. "I'm so sorry for that poor little thing." Then she moved closer to me. "But your aunt's right. She's got to go."

I nodded and gave a sigh that came up from my toes. "You're right," I said. "Darn it."

I'm business manager for TenHuis Chocolade. We produce and sell fabulously delicious bonbons, truffles, and molded chocolate.

My aunt and uncle, Nettie and Phil TenHuis, apprenticed in the chocolate business in Amsterdam forty years ago, then opened their shop in Warner Pier, Michigan, the most picturesque resort on Lake Michigan and their hometown. My uncle Phil died seven years ago, and three years later Aunt Nettie remarried, becoming Nettie TenHuis Jones when she tied the knot with Warner Pier's chief of police, Hogan Jones. She remains president and chief chocolatier at TenHuis.

I handle the money. I'm Lee McKinney Woodyard, from the Texas branch of the family, and I serve as business manager.

Because much of our operation is mail order, we employ people year-round. Many Warner Pier businesses are not able to do that. They focus on the tourist season, from Memorial Day to Labor Day. But TenHuis keeps making truffles and bonbons all winter, fall, and spring. We're not a large operation; we have around thirty-five employees.

And Aunt Nettie refuses to fire a single one of them.

That doesn't mean that TenHuis Chocolade never has an employee who simply does not work out and has to be let go. No, it means that the job of firing people falls to the business manager. I have to do it.

And yes, I hate firing people just as much as Aunt Nettie does. But she's president and sole owner of the company. The Boss. Besides, I owe my dear aunt more than I can ever repay. Twice in my life—when I was sixteen, and my parents got a divorce, and when I was twenty-seven, and I got one myself—she took me in and told me I was going to get through the heartbreak. I love and respect her to the nth degree. I do what she tells me to do.

So if she says, "Take care of it, Lee." I say, "Yes, Aunt Nettie," even if I have to fire somebody. But I don't have to like it.

As if there wasn't enough going on already, I told myself. The regular responsibilities of my job included keeping the accounts, paying the taxes, sending out the bills, supervising our retail shop, ordering supplies, and a million other details. Plus, we were in the middle of preparing for Easter, a major marketing effort for the chocolate business, and my computer had picked this time to act up.

But the biggest problem was that we had launched a remodeling project that was going to double the size of our physical plant. We had bought the building next door, and we were starting the process of adding it to our current building.

The project, of course, was going to require at least twice as much time and twice as much money as we had anticipated. Everybody who had ever been through an expansion project like ours had warned me that would be true. Naturally I hadn't believed them until I was up to my hips in architects.

So I didn't have time to take the bad guy role and fire people. But in the case of Bunny Birdsong, it had to be done that day. Whether I wanted to do it or not.

I considered slashing my wrists. Then I pictured Aunt Nettie's reaction. "Lee, before you go to the hospital to be sewn up, would you please tell Bunny that we're letting her go? While you take care of that, I'll call an ambulance. And try not to bleed into the white chocolate vat."

I couldn't get out of it.

So when Bunny came out of the restroom, I spoke. "Bunny, as soon as you sign in, please come up to my office for a few minutes."

Bunny nodded, though her head drooped even lower. My head was drooping just the same way as I walked up front and sat down behind my desk.

This is not a rehab facility, I told myself. This is a business. Our employees must be productive. If they aren't, then we must replace them. We are not a charity. Our purpose is to make a profit. It's the American way.

Darn it! And darn Joe Woodyard, too! I included my husband in the curse because he had recommended Bunny to us in the first place.

Bunny Birdsong had had a rough time in life. She needed a break for once, and Aunt Nettie and I had hoped we could give her one. But Bunny just hadn't worked out in the chocolate business, even at an entry-level job.

Some people think that low-level workers are dumb or unambitious or lazy or incompetent. That attitude makes me furious. Maybe it's because I come from a blue-collar family, but I have the highest respect for the people who do routine jobs.

I call the ladies who work for TenHuis our "geniuses." They must have great coordination; how many people can swirl a hundred tiny chocolate loops on top of a hundred bonbons and have the hundredth one be as even as the first? How many people can roll a half ounce of nougat into a ball that will become the filling for a truffle, do it two hundred times, and have every single ball be exactly the same weight as all the others? Yes, it's routine work. But it's also highly skilled. And yes, we pay above minimum, and we offer all the benefits we can afford.

But after three months at TenHuis Chocolade, Bunny just wasn't cutting it. Her bonbon decorations were messy. Her truffle production was slow, because she still weighed every single ball of nougat. She had once filled a bowl with milk chocolate and left a trail across the workroom floor when she carried it to the table where she was going to work. And then she stepped in her trail, slipped, and fell down. She could scrub the enrober—a sort of shower bath for truffles and bonbons—until it was spotless, but she could never remember how to reassemble it. After three months, she still required constant supervision.

Then there was this business of being afraid, of thinking someone was trying to hurt her. Bunny was continually fearful. If she got a phone call, there was a weirdo on the line. Her mail was full of crank letters. Or, like today, if she walked down the alley, a strange man followed her.

Yet I liked Bunny. She was sweet. She brought cupcakes—homemade and decorated crookedly—for the break room. She was cheerful, even when things were going askew. She told jokes—silly ones, but endearing. She was interested in her fellow workers. She was kind, and she never gossiped.

She was lovable, but she didn't produce chocolates. All I would be able to do was give her an extra month's salary and promise her a good recommendation.

Darn it again, I thought. Why does life have to be full of bad choices? Bunny's jerk of a husband was divorcing her. She had suddenly faced life without financial support, and now I had to tell her she couldn't handle a routine job making chocolates.

There was no good way to resolve this problem.

My office is in the front of the business so I can oversee the retail shop while I'm working. By the time I was at my desk, I was fit to be tied. So when the phone rang, it didn't help. Especially when the phone call came from one of our more demanding clients.

Stella Drumm is a chief buyer for a major department store chain. She spends a lot of money with us, and she expects a lot of service.

"Lee, I sent you an e-mail yesterday," she said angrily. "Why haven't you answered me?"

"I'm sorry, Stella. I haven't seen an e-mail from you. Can you send me a copy?"

"Never mind. We need to order six thousand eight-inch Easter bunnies in time for a promotion beginning March first. Will that be a problem?"

"Of course not, Stella." Six thousand! I'd get 'em there if I had to make every one myself. An order like that would pay for a lot of electricity and heat.

Stella kept talking. "We want the standard Easter colors, of course. Which reminds me, I hope the colors on your Web page aren't the real colors. Those are lousy. Too harsh. They look like a discount store."

"You're right, Stella. The colors didn't come out well on the Web page. My computer guy is supposed to fix them. I guarantee that the actual bunnies will be decorated with soft pastels."

"They'd better be, or they'll be shipped back to you. Collect. And we want the bunnies divided between the ones with baskets, the ones with wheelbarrows, and the farm boy bunnies with rakes and shovels. Have you got that?"

Yikes, that was going to require a lot of hand decorating, which meant overtime. We could turn the molds—reuse them—only once an hour. I'd have to beg my buddy at the mold company for extras, and they'd have to be sent overnight.

I figured rapidly. "You said two thousand of each?"

"No! We're putting them in a hundred stores. That would be six thousand!"

"Isn't that what you said?"

"No! It's three thousand of each, Lee. Nine thousand."

"I'm sorry I misunderstood." That wasn't what she had said, but for an order that size, I could grovel.

I repeated the order back to her, and she okayed it. She was still snappy, but somewhat mollified.

"I'll send you confirmation immediately," I said. "But I'm concerned because I didn't get your e-mail."

"I sent it through your Web site."

"Oh. We've had some trouble with the Web site. Do you have my regular e-mail?"

Stella and I double-checked to make sure we each had the proper e-mail address. "It's easier to use the Web site," she said.

"I know it is, and I'm going to call the tech immediately to make sure it's working right. If you're having problems, other people may be, too. It gives me the shudders."

We hung up, and I spoke firmly to the computer. "You'd better not cause any problems this Easter," I said. "I have a large mallet in the storeroom with your name on it."

Someone chuckled. I looked up and saw Bunny standing in the doorway. She had added a regulation food-service hairnet since we'd talked earlier. It was crooked, of course.

"Computers are not intimidated by force," she said. "What's this one doing?"

"I've had three cases when people sent me messages through the Web site, and I didn't get them. And our colors aren't true on the Web site."

"That may be your program. What are you using?"

Our conversation grew technical, and immediately I was in over my head. Bunny, however, spoke confidently, advising me to get a new computer program and specifying which one should work. She even sat down at my computer, improved the Web site colors, and tweaked the e-mail function. By the time she got up, I was ready to hug her.

"Bunny! That's great! Why didn't you tell me you knew computer grape juice! I mean, graphics! I didn't know you knew computer graphics."

I am a lifelong sufferer from the affliction called malapropism. We malaprops mix up words with ones that sound similar.

Bunny, like most people who know me well, ignored my goof. She flushed and ducked her head. But she didn't deny her skill.

"Oh, I tried my hand at graphics. I wasn't very good at it. And I know it's really not—you know—art."

"Bunny, is that another one of those things your husband told you?"

She nodded and looked miserable. "Of course, Beau's a real artist. Not just a craftsman."

He was also a real creep, but I didn't mention that. I just tried to be encouraging. "You know, Bunny, there are lots of levels of art—from comic books to Michelangelo. And they all serve a purpose. Just as a lullaby or an aria each has a purpose. You have a very impressive skill with computers, and you should be proud of it."

Bunny smiled sadly. "But right now I need a skill that will pay the rent, and I don't think that TenHuis Chocolade and I are a good mix."

I gulped. That was supposed to be my line. "Why do you say that?"

"When you hired me, you said this was a three-month trial, Lee. My three months are up. So I'll go quietly."

She was echoing what I had planned to say to her. Offering to go. Making it easy for me. But I didn't like it.

I sighed deeply. "Bunny, I'm not going to say you've

been a huge success at making chocolates. But there's something I need even more than a truffle maker, and you just might be it. Would you be interested in a job working on the Web site and handling our e-mail business?"

"Oh!" Bunny's eyes got wide. "I never thought about a job doing that. I don't have any formal training, you know."

"If you think you need some training, we could send you for some."

"You'd do that?"

"If you wanted to go."

"I think I would!" Now Bunny was beaming.

"The bad news is, it's the same salary. And until we get our expansion project finished, you'll have to work in that teeny little closet off the workroom."

"That doesn't matter!" Her expression grew wary. "But would I have to deal with the public?"

"You'd have to answer the phone, and just like everybody else, you might have to sell the occasional bonbon."

"I think I could handle that."

"I know you could."

Bunny and I went around and looked at the tiny closet where her desk would be. It already held a small desk and a chair, and it had computer connections. I promised to call the tech guys we dealt with and ask them to check everything out. "You can talk to them about updating programs, and starting Monday I'll explain what I'm doing with the e-mail orders now."

It was thrilling to see Bunny getting excited about the prospect. This was a solution that suited everyone.

First, I'd gotten a problem employee out of the workroom. Second, I'd hired someone to help me in the office, and Aunt Nettie was always nagging me to do that.

But the third thing was the most important to me. I'd done it without firing anybody. I wanted to click my heels. And I was sure Aunt Nettie was going to be thrilled, too.

So it was a little surprising when she didn't act as excited about my plan as I expected.

We had to talk in my office because even Aunt Nettie doesn't have her own space at the moment. She's a chunky lady with curly white hair, bright Dutch blue eyes, and a sunny smile. But her smile grew cloudy as I described my brilliant idea.

"But, Lee," she said, "what about these delusions that Bunny has?"

"Delusions?"

"You know. The idea that somebody's threatening her."

Chapter 2

Bunny's delusions. Hmmm.

"Maybe we can get her to go to counseling of some sort," I said. But I could hear how weak my voice was when I said it.

"It's a serious problem," Aunt Nettie said. "We can't have that sort of thing disrupting the work, any more than we can live with crooked loops on top of the truffles."

I nodded miserably. "You're right." I sank into a chair beside Aunt Nettie. And "sank" is the right word. I'd been feeling puffed-up proud, and she had punched a thumbtack right in the middle of my ego.

We both sat silently. Then I spoke. "Listen," I said. "I'll talk to Joe tonight. He got us into this—maybe he'll have a suggestion on how to get out. I know, for example, that his agency has referred some of their clients to a therapy group. Or to counselors. Maybe he'll have a suggestion."

We left it at that, and I went back to my desk and began to think about Joe.

My husband, Joe Woodyard, has possibly the most oddball career path of anybody in Michigan. He's an attorney who works in a boat shop.

When Joe tells people that, they blink twice. But he says it's perfect.

Joe—who has dark hair, bright blue eyes, and the best shoulders of any guy in west Michigan—was practically reared in a boat shop.

He was five when his father died in an accident, and his mother, Mercy Woodyard, went to work at an insurance agency. Today she owns it.

While Mercy was busy building a successful career, she relied on her parents to babysit Joe. So Joe grew up with three adults hanging on his every word and action. The one he seems to have been closest to was his grandfather, who owned a boat shop. Joe went there every afternoon as soon as school was out. An occupation that might mean a smashed thumb for many people means home comforts to Joe. Talk to him about shiplap siding or varnish, and he's in heaven. He loves working with his hands, and he loves boats.

In addition to teaching him about boats, Joe says, his grandfather taught him things like honesty, pride in craftsmanship, and "how to be a man." I will testify that Grampa was a good teacher on that last topic.

In addition Joe has the type of intelligence my Texas grandmother called "book smart." He excelled in school academics, athletics, and activities. As a high school senior, he was state wrestling champion in his weight class, captain of the debate team—also state champs—class president, and valedictorian.

If this record is brought up in Joe's presence, he

always says, "There were only forty in my graduating class. That's not a lot of competition." Maybe not, but there was a lot of competition for the scholarship he earned at the University of Michigan.

He went on to law school, and I know Mercy dreamed of seeing Joe as a partner in a major law firm in a large city. Or maybe as a judge. Or in politics. I'm sure the idea of his running for president crossed her mind. She thinks big.

But then Joe handed her a huge disappointment. Instead of seeing law as a way to fame and fortune, he saw it as a way to fight for what's right. He went into poverty law.

I'm sure Mercy cried for a week at the time, but she's come to accept this and even to be proud of him.

Then Joe married the wrong woman, or so he says— the first time around. Joe's former wife was a prominent defense attorney, and he gave up poverty law to join her firm. Their clashes over the purpose and practice of their profession became so heated that Joe not only divorced her, he even divorced his career. He quit practicing law and came back to Warner Pier—to his hometown and his own boat shop.

To sulk, he says.

For refuge, I think. I know how much it hurts to give up on a marriage.

Joe opened Vintage Boats, specializing in the restoration of antique wooden boats. He bought his work clothes at Walmart, instead of from some fancy tailor, and he joined other craftsmen—carpenters, electricians, and machinists—for coffee every morning at the local truck stop. He and I met and cautiously began a love affair.

Then Joe was asked to work one day a week as

Warner Pier city attorney. His hometown needed him, and he eased back into law. Two years later, a law school pal asked him to help start a new poverty law program in Holland, a midsized city thirty miles north of Warner Pier. Joe discovered he still liked poverty law.

So far Joe was happy spending half his workweek as a lawyer for people who needed legal help and couldn't afford it, and the second half restoring antique wooden power boats. He said he found the combination perfect. The days of dealing with legal challenges stimulated him mentally, and the days of working with his hands kept him calm and let his subconscious work on his clients' legal problems.

The guy sounds ideal, right? He's not. He leaves his dirty clothes on the bathroom floor, and he sometimes spends a whole evening staring into space, communicating nothing and not hearing a word I say. Worst of all, if he thinks I'm making a mistake, he tells me about it. What nerve!

Yes, each of us was an only child, and sometimes that's a design for disaster. But most of the time we make it work. And I can always contemplate those shoulders.

Like all of us, Joe wanted the world to run properly, which meant he wanted it to suit him. In particular Joe thought his clients should solve their problems the way he wanted them to. His clients rarely cooperated. Some clients insisted on making unjust wills that left their children at each other's throats. Some of the abused spouses insisted on going back to their abusers. The occasional unemployed father promised to pay more child support than he could afford, when an outsider could see he would never be able to keep his promise.

Sometimes, Joe said, his clients make him want to bang his head against the wall. And Bunny Birdsong was definitely one of the head bangers for Joe. This led her to become a problem to Aunt Nettie and me.

Warner Pier has a highly active art colony, and Bunny's husband, Beau Birdsong, is a well-known member of it. He painted big canvases, usually oils, in bright colors. Critics like him. He shows as far away as Chicago and Detroit. Not in New York and L.A.

Frankly, his work doesn't appeal to me. Too gaudy. But what do I know? I'm an accountant, and to Beau Birdsong I'm just another philistine. To me, Beau is a tall, handsome guy with an amazing pale blond pony-tail and about twice as much personality as he needs.

I had never liked him much, and I liked him even less since he tossed Bunny out.

Joe says that the legal explanation for this action is that Beau is a total jerk. Bunny had, again according to Joe, spent ten years waiting on the guy hand and foot, staying much too busy to hold a job or to finish college or otherwise train for a career. She had finished two years of art school, but she hadn't done as much as a pencil drawing on her own in ten years, and, let's face it, an art career almost always requires a day job to buy groceries.

When Beau took up with a dramatic brunet and told Bunny their marriage was over, she left home with twenty dollars in her pocket. No car, no clothes, no relatives, and no close friends; he'd kept her too busy to develop those.

So Bunny wound up at the poverty law center. Joe got her some temporary financial support and found her a place to stay in the Holland shelter for abused women.

But Bunny had lived in Warner Pier a long time. And she had no transportation. Warner Pier is small; you can walk anyplace in town. Bunny wanted to stay here.

So when I mentioned that TenHuis Chocolade was thinking of hiring a couple of people, Joe put in a good word for Bunny.

So maybe it's not fair for me to blame Joe for the addition of Bunny to our staff. He had only mentioned her name and angrily told me how badly her husband was treating her. I admit I was the one who hired her. Her story made me feel sorry for her, and the job didn't demand a high level of skill. I thought almost anyone could do it.

Except it turned out that Bunny, despite two years of art school, was not well coordinated. She dropped things, broke things, and spilled things. Plus, she kept telling us this nonsensical story about how some person she'd never seen before was chasing her, even trying to kill her. And I felt too sorry for her simply to fire her.

So maybe I was the head banger. Not Joe. Not Bunny. I really had no one to blame but myself. But maybe Joe could suggest a counselor who could help Bunny.

I was jotting down a few points I wanted to make about Bunny when the second wave of Birdsongs attacked. Loudly.

I looked up to see what the noise was about. A tall woman was standing in front of the cash register. "I want to talk to Mrs. Birdsong," she said. Her voice reverberated through the shop. "I'm her aunt, and I need to discuss a family matter with her."

The counter girl—Janie Burke—looked both angry and terrified.

"I'll see if Bunny is available," she said. Then she looked at me. After all, I'm in charge of the front counter.

I nodded. "It's all right, Janie," I said. "I think Bunny's in the little room off the workshop. Just ask her to step up front."

Janie dashed for the back, and I eyeballed Bunny's visitor. She was sixtyish, with permed gray hair. A sprig of plastic holly was stuck in one side of her knit cap. Since Christmas was past, it gave her a crazy look. Her chin was firm; it kept her from looking friendly or attractive. She wore the Warner Pier winter uniform: a ski jacket, coordinating pants, and heavy boots. Hers looked expensive. She was gawking around the shop as if she were thinking of buying it. Not buying chocolates. Buying the shop.

Janie returned with Bunny. Bunny looked almost as terrified as Janie had.

"Hello, Aunt Abigail," she said. "I didn't know you were in town."

"And I didn't know that you had left Beau," she said. "There's never been anything like this in the Birdsong family. What were you thinking?"

If Bunny had looked terrified before, now she looked completely stricken. That's when I decided to interfere in Bunny's affairs. There was, after all, no need for them to become the whole town's affairs, as they would be if Bunny and her aunt discussed things in the shop.

I got to my feet and called out, "Bunny! If you and your visitor need to talk, you can take her back to your new office."

Bunny fled back to her little cubbyhole, followed by the loud woman. I got up and closed my door. I stared at the intercom on my desk for at least a full minute.

Then I gave in to temptation and turned it on. After all, I told myself, I might need to step in and help Bunny. Plus, this aunt had been ready to discuss their "family matter" in the shop itself, in front of Janie Burke and the ladies who make the chocolates and any customers who came in.

I turned the intercom down to the lowest setting. Aunt Abby was speaking as it began to broadcast. "And you've moved out? I was told you were renting a room from Clara Vanderberg! What is going on?"

"I couldn't stay at our house after Beau told me to get out."

"Pish, tush. Come, come. You know Beau's rude when he's working. But it doesn't mean anything."

"But he moved another woman in."

Somebody gave a loud gasp. It had to be Aunt Abby. "My dear! That is simply impossible. I'm sure you misunderstood their relationship."

"It would have been pretty hard to misunderstand."

Aunt Abby lowered her voice. "He must have been drinking. I'm sure nothing really happened."

"Aunt Abigail . . ."

"You should know Beau by now."

"Beau told me to get out. So I left."

"I'm sure that it's all a misunderstanding, my dear. I'll talk to Beau."

"No." Bunny's voice was weak.

"I'll straighten him out, Bunny. There'll be no more behavior like that."

"No." Bunny's voice was even weaker.

"I know you love Beau. He'll toe the line."

"No."

I heard the door to Bunny's cubbyhole open, and I

switched the intercom off. Then I opened the door to my own office.

Aunt Abigail came steaming out of the workroom like a Lake Michigan freighter. "I'll take care of the whole matter, Bunny," she said.

"No!" Now Bunny sounded anguished.

"Oh yes! I'll fix that young man. He'll understand his responsibilities. This misunderstanding will be completely forgotten."

"No! Aunt Abigail! I don't care what Beau does!"

The woman turned on her heel and faced Bunny. She patted the younger woman on her hand. "My dear! I know how to settle Beau's hash. I'll simply tell him that because he's treated you so badly, he's no longer my heir. I'll call my lawyer immediately and make an appointment for tomorrow. I'm changing my will. Beau will get nothing. All my money will go to you."

She sailed out the door.

Bunny stood in the middle of the shop. Tears were running down her cheeks. When I went to her, patted her on the shoulder, and made what I hoped were comforting sounds, she cried even harder.

Behind her I could see Janie Burke. She was glaring at the front door, the door through which this Aunt Abby had gone a moment before.

The look on her face would have shattered granite rock into gravel.

Chapter 3

Since my office has no privacy, I took Bunny—and a box of Kleenex—back to her cubbyhole and sat her on the chair. I perched on the tiny desk while she blew her nose.

"I'm sorry to make a scene, Lee."

"It wasn't your fault. Bunny, who was that woman?"

"I thought everybody in Warner Pier knew her."

"I've lived here more than four years, but I'm still a newcomer."

"She's Beau's aunt. His father's sister. Abigail Birdsong. She owns one of those big houses in Shorefront."

"Oh." I understood. Shorefront is one of the nicer neighborhoods.

Warner Pier has three social classes—locals, tourists, and summer people. Locals live here all year round. Tourists stay for a few days or a couple of weeks. Summer people own cottages and stay for most of the summer.

Shorefront is an old addition of summer cottages—and in Shorefront a "cottage" may be the size of a mansion. Families with property in Shorefront are likely to have been visiting Warner Pier for a hundred years or more. We locals run things, in a sense, because we vote here. But summer people tend to have the status lent by "old money," education, and rank. And as out-of-state property owners, they pay big taxes here. Financially, we locals love them.

Bunny sighed. "Aunt Abigail thinks Beau is wonderful. She admires his 'artistic temperament.'"

"My family called that 'childish sulking,' but none of us were artistic."

"I don't think any of the Birdsongs were artistic either," Bunny said. "Aunt Abigail wishes they had been, I guess. She's always sponsoring art shows."

"You and Beau have been separated for more than four months, but she didn't seem to know about it. Where's she been?"

Before Bunny could answer, I clapped my hand over my mouth. She looked surprised. So I took the hand down. "Sorry, Bunny. This is none of my business. You certainly don't need to explain anything to me."

"I don't mind talking about it. Abigail only comes to Warner Pier in the summer. I thought maybe that Beau brought up all this divorce business at Halloween thinking that we could get it over with before she found out."

I didn't comment. She was probably right.

Bunny dried a few tears and gave a timid smile. "I never thought I'd feel like this."

"Like what?"

"When Aunt Abigail started her tirade, I realized I'm glad that Beau is out of my life."

"You are?"

"Yes! And I'm so surprised. I met him in art school. I thought he was wonderful. For ten years I lived with that 'artistic temperament.' I was proud to be his wife."

"Artists have a certain status in Warner Pier— anywhere, I guess. Even if they have that temperament."

"When Beau told me our marriage was over, I thought I'd die. Now I see that I spent the past ten years acting like a fool. It's such a relief to know I don't have to put up with him anymore!"

"So when his aunt says she'll speak to him about your marriage . . ."

"Oh, Lee, I hope he doesn't listen to her!"

"But even if he does, Bunny, you don't have to go back to him."

"I know. I know. But I'm not sure I can stand up to the two of them."

"Aunt Abigail and Beau?"

"Right. They've bossed me around for so long."

"You told Aunt Abigail 'no.' Repeatedly."

"And she paid no attention to me."

I nodded. "I noticed that."

"I'm afraid . . ." Bunny stopped talking and wiped away more tears. "I wish I could be like you, Lee. Strong."

I saw my opportunity, and I jumped in. "Believe me, Bunny, if I appear strong, it's because I spent five years not being strong."

Bunny looked suitably amazed.

"I had a bad first marriage. I won't go into details, but I spent a lot of time doing things I didn't want to do because I thought that it would keep peace. It took a long time with a counselor before I saw that no matter how hard I tried, I was never going to be happy. And my husband wasn't going to be happy either, because he was living with an unhappy woman. I learned to stand up for myself. You can, too."

"Do you think I could? I can't afford a counselor."

"I think Joe knows some who charge on the basis of ability to pay. Why don't you ask him about it?"

"I guess I could."

"And in the meantime, just keep saying 'no' if you want to. Besides, it was Beau who ended your marriage. Even if his aunt doesn't approve, why would he listen to her?"

Bunny gave a weak smile. "It's the money."

I had the sense not to reply to that. But it gave me something to think about as I went back to my office. Then I resolved to push Bunny's affairs out of my mind. Do your own work, I told myself firmly. You have plenty. If you're going to break Bunny in to a new job starting Monday, you have to have your own desk cleared today.

The only interruption came from Janie Burke, who brought me the credit card records. Her face was still like a thundercloud.

"What's wrong, Janie?" I asked.

"Nothing, Lee."

"You're usually a little ray of sunshine around here, and this afternoon—not so much. Is something wrong?"

"Not on the job. I mean, I've got to work someplace, and this is as good as any."

"I'm glad to hear that." I knew Janie had graduated from Warner Pier High School the previous June and had come to us looking for a summer job. When Labor Day came, she asked to stay on. She was a good worker, but I'd noticed a slight dissatisfaction with working in the chocolate world and minding a cash register.

I guess that Janie had caught my sarcastic tone,

because she looked dismayed and plunked down into my visitor's chair. "I'm sorry, Lee! I didn't mean to sound so rotten."

"You're a good worker, Janie. As long as you don't sound rotten to the customers, I have no complaints. Did something happen today that made you feel bad?"

"Oh, it's that lousy Miss Birdsong. She got my father fired. And I had to skip college for a year at least."

"I don't blame you for resenting her. What did she do to your father?"

"He was the caretaker for her cottage. He opened it and closed it and did minor repairs. She got mad at him; claimed he had stolen a piece of antique furniture! He did not do that! And she never even accused him to his face. She just bad-mouthed him all over the neighborhood. She cost him half his clients."

"That's awful!" And it was awful. A caretaker like Janie's dad would have the keys to cottages whose worth added up to several million dollars. Yes, he had to be trustworthy. To be blamed for something he didn't do, but never have a chance to stand up for himself— it would be infuriating. And it could send his business into bankruptcy. And it could mean that his daughter had to drop her college plans and work for slightly more than minimum in a chocolate shop.

Bummer.

I assured Janie that if I heard of any repair or maintenance work, I'd recommend her dad. Then I told her that summer work at TenHuis had helped me get jobs that saw me through college.

She went back to the cash register a little more cheerful. But I knew that her anger at Abigail Birdsong wasn't gone.

I resolved to keep working on my own job. I kept

my resolve for nearly an hour, clearing my correspondence, sorting bills, and adding up some sales figures. I called the tech who tends our computers—asking him to come over Monday and set up the computer in Bunny's office. So I'd accomplished a few things by the time the third attack of the Birdsongs happened. Beau Birdsong walked in.

He gave his usual broad, lady-killing smile and headed for my office. I was sure Beau had nothing to say to me, but he always has to swagger a little when he's around a woman. Any woman.

Beau was a handsome man—tall and slim, with finely chiseled features. And he had waist-length, very light blond hair, worn in that famous ponytail. And he had brown eyes. Dark eyes combined with fair hair can be devastating, and I fear that a lot of hearts have been broken by Beau's unusual coloring.

In a town the size of Warner Pier, everybody knows everybody, so Joe and I often ran into Beau Birdsong on a casual basis. He's Mr. Popularity with a lot of people. Like I said, I had never liked him, though I hadn't cared enough to figure out why. Finally Joe explained his own take on my dislike.

"You're jealous of Beau because his ponytail is as pretty as yours," he said.

After we both stopped laughing, I admitted that might be a factor. I have thick white-blond hair, courtesy of the Dutch side of my family, and from the time I was a child people told me it was pretty. And Joe was right; Beau's ponytail was longer, thicker, and maybe glossier than mine. Plus, I had the accompanying Curse of the Blonde—invisible lashes that make my eyes disappear. Beau, however, had those dark eyelashes and eyebrows. Killer.

I didn't waste time envying Beau his eyelashes. I just got mine dyed every month. And my eyes, or so Joe says, are a nice shade of hazel that verges on green. But Beau's dark eyes, almost black, contrasting with his long blond hair, were really eye-catching.

Since I learned how he'd browbeaten Bunny, I had a double dislike of Beau. It cost me a lot of effort to act pleasant as he walked toward my office.

He was wearing a dashing hat with one side of the brim pinned up, as if he were out on a kangaroo hunt. When he got to the door of my office, he swept the hat off.

"Hello, Lee. You're looking gorgeous today."

I couldn't resist. "You are, too, Beau. Can I help you?"

"Actually I'll try not to bother you. I need to talk to Bunny for just a moment." He grimaced charmingly. "Some of our legal problems."

"I'll see if she's available. Please wait here."

I got to my feet and edged past Beau, who wasn't giving me much room to go around him. I turned into the workroom and looked into the little cubbyhole where Bunny had been working.

It was empty. So I scanned the workroom. No sign of her.

"Looking for Bunny?" Dolly Jolly was close enough to me that she didn't need to yell, but she did it anyway.

"Yes. She has a caller."

"She just went out the back door! I sent her on an errand!"

I was a bit surprised. Then Dolly gave me a broad wink and jerked her head toward the front. I deduced that Bunny hadn't wanted to see Beau.

"Okay," I said. I returned to the shop and told Beau that his ex was out. No, I didn't know how long she would be gone.

He looked pained, of course. Beau would look pained, no matter what. I recognized it as a play for sympathy.

"May I give her a message?" I asked.

"No, thanks," Beau said slowly. "A situation has arisen . . . Well, ask her to call me."

He was still standing there when the door swung open again, and someone spoke.

"Oh good. Beau!"

I immediately knew who had come in. It was Beau's girlfriend, Anya Hartley. When I looked up I saw that she was followed by her brother, Andrew Hartley. I couldn't pretend I didn't know them, not in a town the size of Warner Pier.

Golly gee, I thought. The gang's all here. I hoped that they weren't all going to yell at one another. Anya's artistic temperament was as famous as Beau's.

Anya was what is commonly known as a stunner. She had enough long, dark hair to knit into a sweater. Her eyes were a light, clear blue, like limpid pools—or that's what I'd heard Beau tell someone in describing her. Her features were bold and well shaped. And she was tall, with plenty of bosom and bottom.

Frankly, I didn't think she would age well. She was large scale all over. Not fat. She simply looked a little too lush. As an artist, she worked in tempera, splashing it into patterns of jungles, exotic waterfalls, and other imaginary landscapes as lush as she was herself.

Andrew was tall and thin, much less showy than his sister. He had hair as dark as hers, but his was thinning. He wore glasses with dark frames. He almost disappeared behind his lack of personality. Until he smiled. He had a truly sweet smile. A very likable guy.

Andrew was also an artist, in his case creating tiny wood carvings of birds. Itsy-bitsy gulls, robins, sparrows, and ducks, delicately painted to match nature, were his specialty. His day job—as a proper artist, he had a day job—was managing the wine shop next door to TenHuis. Anya worked for him, irregularly.

Andrew hung back, trailing behind Anya.

Anya walked up to Beau and patted his chest. "There you are. I need twenty dollars."

"I thought you were going to use the Visa."

"Oh, the stupid machine didn't like it."

Huh. As a merchant I knew what that probably meant: maxed out. But I tried not to change my expression as I finished writing the note asking Bunny to call Beau. "I'll make sure Bunny gets this," I said.

"Oh, thanks, Lee," Beau answered absently and kept digging through his pockets. He pulled out a five and two ones, then frowned at Anya. "This is all the change I've got. You know I rarely carry money."

"I know you rarely *have* any." Her voice was annoyed. "Well, it's a darling top. I'll go back and tell them to hold it for me."

"You just got a new outfit yesterday." Beau sounded annoyed.

Anya glared. Her lip curled, and she opened her mouth. Before she could speak, I jumped in. "Beau, Anya, Andrew—may I offer each of you a chocolate?"

Chocolate can solve any problem. My offer distracted them, and we moved over to the display counter. Anya selected a Café Raspberry truffle ("milk chocolate center enrobed with dark chocolate and embellished with pink stripes") and Beau went for a Chocolate Cheesecake truffle ("white chocolate center covered in dark chocolate, centered with a white dot"). Andrew hung back until I insisted that he choose a treat, then selected a French vanilla ("milk chocolate ganache and shell, decorated with crumbled white chocolate"). He smiled as he said thanks, and I was again surprised at how his face warmed.

Anya barely thanked me. She spoke to Beau. "Let's go, darling. You know how arguing about money tires me out."

But they weren't to escape. Before they could get to the door, it swung open again and—ta-da!—the fourth invasion happened. Aunt Abigail was back.

"Beau!" She spoke harshly. "What's this drivel I hear about you and Bunny splitting up?"

Then she proceeded to pound Beau into the ground. All he could say was, "Yes, Aunt Abigail," and "No, Aunt Abigail."

Wimp. Total wimp. If Beau was getting money from his aunt—and I didn't know that he was—he was earning it the hard way. I would never have put up with a scolding like that one from anyone. And in public.

I thought Abigail Birdsong was never going to run out of breath, but she finally did come to a stop.

Then Anya started, lashing into Abigail Birdsong. "How dare you talk to Beau like that! We love each other. Bunny has to step aside!"

Anya took off like a jet plane, and she really let Abigail have it. Abigail, naturally, responded. And her first line was, "And who are you?"

The two of them put on quite a show. And they had quite an audience. Aunt Nettie came out, clicking her tongue. All the ladies gathered round the door from the workshop. I sat at my desk staring. A customer actually opened the street door, took one look, turned, and ran down the street.

Beau stood there muttering ineffectually. "Aunt Abigail, please." And "Anya, this is not a good idea." They both ignored him. Andrew effaced himself, standing against the wall. He kept edging toward the street door, but he couldn't get by Anya and Abigail.

Finally Beau did the right thing. He put his hat on, pushed past the two women, and left.

Smart man. I wished I could go with him.

Andrew tried to go along, but he was still boxed in.

My aunt Nettie was the only person who didn't lose her head. She walked over to Abigail Birdsong, patted her on the arm, and very quietly spoke. "Abigail, this isn't accomplishing anything."

Abigail stopped talking in the middle of a sentence.

I copied Aunt Nettie's actions, going to Anya. I put my arm around her shoulder and said, "Anya." I tried to use my softest voice. "Come to the back with me, Anya."

I used my arm to turn her, and to my surprise she came along. She stopped talking, too. I realized we had abandoned Andrew, so I turned and beckoned for him to follow.

"Come along, Andrew," I said.

First Andrew gave a little bow, facing Aunt Abigail.

"I have to get back to the wine shop," he said. "I won't be free until it closes at nine."

Then he followed me, almost tiptoeing.

Abigail watched us go. First she gasped, then she looked astonished. She raised a hand, and for a moment I thought she was going to speak. Then she seemed to give up.

Silence fell as we entered the workroom. But it was broken by Abigail's voice from the front. "Nettie, I apologize. I've disrupted your business. I must leave now at any rate. I have an important appointment in Holland."

I remember thinking, as I guided Anya along, that it was already four o'clock, rather late for an appointment in Holland, which was thirty minutes away. But the thought flitted out of my brain as quickly as it had come in. I concentrated on getting Anya calmed down. It took about fifteen minutes to accomplish that and send her on her way. To my surprise Andrew joined in on my side, speaking calmly to Anya and urging her not to argue with Abigail Birdsong again.

"She's old, Anya," he said. "Don't waste your breath."

Anya and Andrew finally exited through the alley door. I took a quick look to make sure they wouldn't meet Bunny. Or Aunt Abigail.

Then Aunt Nettie came back to the break room. She and I looked at each other, shaking our heads.

"I don't know if I should laugh or cry," she said.

"Let's laugh," I said.

So we did. We each got a really good chocolate— mine had a soft caramel filling (milk chocolate–flavored caramel enrobed in dark chocolate and embellished with a milk chocolate C). That and a cup of coffee and a good laugh at the strangeness of human nature fixed us both up.

Of course, since it had happened in front of twenty-five women who were all locals, the tale of the Anya versus Abigail quarrel was all over town in about twenty minutes. I didn't tell anybody but Joe. He and I had another good laugh over it.

But I quit laughing the next morning, when disaster hit our remodeling project.

Who's Who in Chocolate

CHRISTOPHER COLUMBUS

Christopher Columbus discovered America—or so it's generally thought. I'm not getting into *that* controversy. But did he discover chocolate?

The first mention of chocolate in European writings comes in an account of Columbus's fourth voyage, an account written by Columbus's son Ferdinand.

On August 15, 1502, Ferdinand wrote, off the island of Guanaja, forty miles north of Honduras, a reconnaissance party captured a large dugout canoe rowed by slaves. In it were all sorts of trading goods—cloth, foods, copper war clubs, plus other things. Among the goods were what appeared to be some special "almonds." The Spanish noted that these "almonds" were highly valued by the people they had captured.

Later the Spanish discovered that these were used for money and even later that the "almonds" were made into a bitter drink, which could be flavored with hot peppers. Eventually some "almonds" were sent back to Spain, where no one was particularly impressed.

Chapter 4

I was the one who fell into the disaster. And all I was doing was being conscientious. Or maybe nosy.

When a building is being remodeled, one of the problems is keeping track of what's going on with the construction without getting in the way.

Six months earlier TenHuis Chocolade had bought the building next door. It had previously been occupied by a business aimed at the tourist trade, a gift and novelties shop with the theme of clowns. The store had offered clown costumes, clown tricks, clown books, clown cards, clown candy, clown makeup, and any other clown paraphernalia manufactured. The owner had even performed as a clown.

After his unfortunate demise, his family put the building up for sale, and Aunt Nettie, with urging from her niece and business manager, had purchased the structure. Because of its history, we all still called it the Clown Building.

It wasn't very fancy. Like much of the downtown of Warner Pier, the narrow brick structure had been put up in the last decade of the 1800s. It hadn't been kept up well during much of its hundred-plus years. When we got it, it had needed new wiring, a new roof, new plumbing, new everything. The building was going to double the size of TenHuis Chocolade—and we did need the room—but making the Clown Building useful was going to require a lot of work.

We were just getting started on the project. The only part of the work that was finished so far was updating the apartment upstairs. In a resort town like Warner Pier, nearly all the downtown buildings have apartments upstairs. These are usually rented by summer workers—sometimes year-round workers—and provide a little extra income to the building owners. The previous fall Joe and I had taken off from our respective jobs for a week and completely redone the four-room apartment in the Clown Building. A very pretty girl named Chayslee Brett Zimmerman now lived there. She worked for a downtown restaurant. Not as a waitress. No, Chayslee was a chef.

Aunt Nettie was the official owner of the property, of course, but as her representative, I was in charge of spending a lot of the money. I was responsible for seeing that the renovation went according to plan and for making sure that the plans were going to work. If the tile wasn't the right color or a door opened the wrong way, I had to see that the problem was corrected.

So I needed to tour the place every day, or so I thought, and I tried to do it at a time when I wouldn't annoy the workmen. But most days the workmen came around seven thirty or eight. I wasn't so devoted to my job that I showed up at six a.m. so I could look around before they came. Instead I often made a tour at lunchtime. But on Saturdays, when no workmen were there, or at least very few of them, I tried to do a longer walk-through early in the day.

That was my excuse for showing up that morning.

I had parked on the street, next to the pickup of one of the construction crew chiefs, Mike Westerly.

Mike and I often arrived around the same time. He was a burly guy, at least six foot four, with hair as red as Dolly Jolly's. In contrast with his striking appearance—huge guy with bright red hair—he spoke very quietly. I always had to try hard to hear him.

"Can you get in through the front, Mike?" I asked. "If not, you can cut through our building."

I could see Mike's lips move, but as usual I could barely hear his voice. "I have a key," he said.

The whole front of the Clown Building was currently gone. Mike put on his orange hard hat and opened a makeshift door in the boarded-up front. I opened the street door at TenHuis Chocolade, went in, and locked the door behind myself. We wouldn't be admitting customers until ten o'clock.

I'd barely hung up my jacket when the yelling started in back of the building.

The only people expected there that day were the construction workers, so my first fear was that some sort of accident had occurred. Choosing the quickest way to the sound, I ran through our workroom and break room, opened the alley door, and peeked around it. Mike was standing in the alley, and he seemed to be looking directly at me.

"Hey! Hey! Come see!" His soft voice was gone. Now his shouts were echoing off the brick walls that lined the alley.

Mike had walked through the building and changed from a calm, almost sleepy guy to one who was close to panic.

"Jack! There's a dead body in here!"

I realized Mike was calling for the contractor, Jack VanSickle.

A dead body? In the Clown Building? I couldn't take it in. I stepped out the door and turned into the alley, determined to figure out what was going on.

A voice came from behind me. "Anybody we know?"

I turned to see Jack VanSickle walking down the alley toward me.

In contrast to Mike, VanSickle looked calm, as if he found a dead body every morning when he showed up for work.

"It's not a homeless guy," Mike said.

I'd been told that homeless people sometimes broke into construction sites, maybe because they weren't always securely locked up. So I guess that had been Mike's first expectation.

He spoke again. "It's some old gal."

"Does she need CPR?" Jack asked.

"Too late for that."

Still acting cool, Jack gave me a casual nod as he passed, and I followed him over to the Clown Building's back door. He and Mike went in the door and knelt about ten feet inside. It was not very light there, but I could see that they were staring at a heap of blue and black fabric. This was apparently the body. I could see the soles of a pair of boots, side by side, with the toes flopped out limply. But I couldn't see a face. The body was lying absolutely flat on its back.

Neither Jack nor Mike said anything. Then Jack reached in his pocket and brought out a cell phone.

He hit three keys and spoke to the 9-1-1 operator, reporting the discovery.

"We'll wait outside," he told the phone. "No, it doesn't look like a homeless guy. It's an older woman, nice jacket, warm clothes. But I don't recognize her."

I couldn't resist. I walked in the back door and approached the body closely enough to see the face. I guess I gasped, because both Jack and Mike looked up at me.

My voice was a whisper when I spoke again.

"It's Abigail Birdsong," I said. "What else can harpoon? I mean, happen!"

My twisted tongue had tripped me up again. I tried to ignore it.

I think I just stood there, my mouth gaping. I know I felt as if I'd been hit by one of the two-by-fours that were lying around the site. Hit right in the head.

Jack VanSickle and Mike gently pulled me out the back door, muttering about law enforcement and other important factors. I didn't argue; they were perfectly right. I offered to let them wait inside our back door where it was a bit warmer, but they shook their heads and zipped their jackets.

"The cops won't be long," VanSickle said.

"I'll leave our back door unlocked," I said. "Come in if y'all change your minds." Then I went into our break room, made a pot of coffee, and thought. My heart was pounding and my head spinning.

How on earth had Abigail Birdsong wound up dead, and what was her body doing in the Clown Building?

And what had happened to her? Did she drop dead of a heart attack? Keel over from a stroke? My glimpse of her had shown no sign that she had died by violence. There was no blood, for example. But if she simply died of natural causes, why was she laid out neatly on the floor of the Clown Building? That made no sense.

Unlike the loosely secured type of construction site that invites the homeless or other prowlers, the Clown Building was locked up tight when everyone left. The front door, the back door, and the door into our building—all were tightly secured every night.

Had Mrs. Birdsong been moved into the Clown Building after she was dead? That would probably make it homicide.

And what should I do? Should I call Beau? Was he Abigail's closest relative? But Abigail seemed to be friendlier to Bunny. Should I call her instead?

I definitely felt that I should Do Something—with capital letters. I mean, a body had been discovered on property I was responsible for. I needed to react. Didn't I? Or did I?

And what about witnesses? A lot of the apartments in our block were empty for the winter, but Dolly Jolly lived over TenHuis, the pretty Chayslee lived over the Clown Building, and Andrew Hartley lived over the wine shop where he was manager. Was it possible that some of them had seen something?

My thoughts were tumbling around. Then I heard a siren in the alley and peeked out to see a Warner Pier police car pull in. It was the one with CHIEF OF POLICE painted on the doors. This, of course, made me think of the building's official owner: my aunt, who was the wife of the chief of police.

"Aunt Nettie needs to know about this," I said aloud. "If she doesn't already know." Hogan might have told her.

I poured myself a cup of the coffee I'd made, took five deep breaths, and called her.

As usual, she took the crisis calmly. Aunt Nettie looks sweet and gentle, as if a strong blast from a fan might knock her over. Actually she can withstand a hurricane. When I told her that a prominent local citizen had been found dead in our building, all she said was, "My goodness."

Then she added, "I guess that explains why Hogan ran out of here so quickly."

I realized that being married to the police chief—as Aunt Nettie was—had certain advantages. She might well know more about the situation than I did. But her next words shattered that illusion. "Have you seen him?"

Obviously Hogan hadn't taken time to tell her about the body on her property before he left.

"I think Hogan's here," I said. "Of course, I know better than to get in his way."

"Me, too."

We were both lying, of course. We'd been known not only to get in Hogan's way, but even to cause him quite a bit of annoyance. But that morning I was trying to be good.

Aunt Nettie spoke again. "I'll be there in twenty minutes," she said.

I also called Joe, and he came down, his hair still wet from the shower. I filled both Aunt Nettie, when she arrived, and Joe in on what I'd seen in the Clown Building. Then we sat. And we sat.

Oh, something happened now and then. Hogan came in through our back door once, for example, and looked at the padlock that held the door between our shop and the Clown Building closed. He also asked us not to tell anyone who the victim was. The van that held the crime lab from the Michigan State Police showed up; its crew assists small municipalities such as Warner Pier with investigations. They went into the Clown Building and began their exotic activities with tape measures and cameras and the more complicated equipment they used.

Then the phone began to ring.

Warner Pier is a small town, after all. People wanted to know why we had police on the premises. The banker, the baker, the baby doll maker—they all called to find out what was going on.

As Hogan had asked, all Aunt Nettie and I said was that a body had been discovered by workmen that morning. Police were investigating. That was all we knew, we lied.

I did spot Mike at one point, sitting in his pickup truck in front of our shop, and I went out to ask one question.

But he asked me one first. "That Ms. Jolly—is she all right?"

"I'll check," I said. "But I think she was going out of town this weekend."

Mike looked relieved. He didn't ask anything else. So I asked my question. Was the back door of the Clown Building locked when he came that morning?

Mike assured me that the heavy padlock on the alley door had been in place.

"I'd seen Jack turn into the alley," he said. "I nearly fell over that old gal when I walked through. I had to unlock the back door to call Jack."

I thanked him, but Mike's answer left me with a question: How had either Abigail Birdsong or her killer (if she'd been killed) gotten into the building?

Of course, the Clown Building could be entered from the TenHuis Building. But the alley door to

TenHuis Chocolade was held by two solid locks, one in the door handle and a second, a dead bolt, above it. On the front, the building's street door led into our retail shop, and that door was also locked.

Normally show windows lined the fronts of both buildings, though the Clown Building was boarded up at the moment. The simplest way to break into either building would be to knock out a window in our building and climb through, then cut a hole in the temporary partition separating us from the Clown Building.

In Michigan, in winter, I can guarantee, a hole in the window would be noticed immediately, simply because of the draft.

There was a temporary door linking the TenHuis side and the Clown Building side. It was held shut by a sturdy padlock hooked through a heavy hasp. It would take a pry bar of some sort to get that hasp off, and the first person in for work at TenHuis would notice the resulting damage.

I checked; the padlock was in place and was still locked.

We had tried to make it all secure. So how did someone get into the Clown Building without leaving evidence of how they did it? I hoped the police knew.

I remembered a conversation with Jack VanSickle when work first began. A lot of people would be going in and out, he said.

"We'll need to secure your side of the building, to keep your equipment and stock safe," he told me. "But it's not easy to keep a construction site locked up. Especially one on a city street. Not with an alley like this one."

"Surely you can board up the front of the Clown Building," I said.

"The front isn't the problem. The problem is the number of people coming in and out, both front and back."

"Padlocks and keys?"

"It would take a dozen or more. Too many to control. So until we get the back and front of this building walled in and can install good doors, I'm going to limit access from the current building to the Clown Building to one door, and I'm going to close that door with a solid bolt." And he had done that.

Eventually the wall between the buildings—actually walls, one for each building, shoulder to shoulder—would be taken down. Pillars would be left to hold up the second floors, but there would be open spaces between the pillars. But while the new building, the former Clown Building, was being gutted, the area between the buildings was solidly locked. Or so we thought.

As we waited that morning, Joe kept wandering in and out, trying to keep an eye on whatever was happening next door. This wasn't an easy chore, since he couldn't go into the building.

Aunt Nettie and I got tired of hearing the phone ring, and I pulled the plugs of the front office, retail store, and break room extensions. Joe had stepped outside again, and Aunt Nettie and I were sitting in my office, both of us in states of near unconsciousness, when a new noise began.

We both jumped. "Someone is banging on the front door," Aunt Nettie said.

I went to the glass door and peeked behind the shade.

"It's Bunny," I said. "I guess I'd better let her in."

"Okay," Aunt Nettie said. "But don't tell her her aunt's dead. Hogan needs to handle that."

I unlocked the door and opened it. Bunny rushed in. "Lee! Mrs. Jones! Why are all the police back in the alley? What's happened?"

She looked frantic. She looked so frantic that I tried hard to look and sound calm when I answered her.

"The early workmen found a body in the Clown Building," I said. "The police are here. We don't know much yet."

"Oh my gosh!" Bunny's voice was anything but calm. "In the Clown Building?"

"Right."

"Oh golly! And just think. I was over there last night."

Chapter 5

I'm sure I gasped before I spoke. "You were over there last night? What on earth for?"

"Hiding out, I guess. I saw Aunt Abigail's car on the street, and she got out and started looking around. I didn't want to talk to her because I was really upset over her threats."

"Her threats?"

"Yes. The idea that she might demand that Beau and I get back together."

I considered that. I couldn't see why Bunny considered that a threat. After all, she could always say no. Even admitting that Bunny had trouble saying either yes or no . . . surely she wouldn't let a third party influence her marital life. That would be freaky. I tried to shove the idea aside.

"In any case you'll have to talk to Hogan," I said. "They'll be looking for anybody who was around the Clown Building last night. As a witness."

I considered that remark for a full minute, then I spoke again. "And maybe you need to talk to Joe before you see Hogan."

Yes, I was sure Joe would want to talk to Bunny before she spoke to Hogan. After all, Joe was Bunny's lawyer, at least for her divorce. And it was beginning to sound as if she would need a lawyer. But Joe had left the building, gone someplace. I didn't know where he was, though it probably wasn't very far away. I reached for my cell phone.

Bunny ignored my remark about Joe. "So there was a murder there? At the Clown Building?"

Aunt Nettie and I looked at each other. "We don't know yet if it was a murder or not," Aunt Nettie said. "Just that a body was found there this morning."

Bunny shook her head. But she didn't ask any more questions. It didn't seem to occur to Bunny that the victim could be anybody she knew.

I called Joe's cell phone. Naturally, since I really needed him, his phone was off. I left a message on his voice mail and turned back to Bunny. Yes, I decided, she needed to have Joe present when she talked to Hogan. Even if she didn't know a single thing about Abigail Birdsong's death, Bunny was the type of person who would blurt out something that would send her up the river.

As if to confirm my opinion, Bunny came a few steps farther into the office and tripped over a chair. She caught herself on its back, so she didn't land on the floor, but she dropped her purse. All the contents, including a cell phone, three ballpoint pens, a coin purse, and a luxurious notebook—the kind with a gold foil cover—fell out. The coin purse had apparently been left unzipped; change showered over the shop floor.

I sighed and got down on my knees to help her pick it up. Bunny apologized the whole time we were scrambling for the coins, acting as if I were going to punish her for the accident.

As soon as the change had ceased to be a threat to anyone walking around in our shop, I went to the alley door. The alley was crowded with cops and detectives and their vehicles, including the scientific van. There was a regular throng back there.

I called to a patrolman walking by. It was Jerry Cherry—midthirties and as burly as the red-haired construction worker who had raised the original alarm. I knew Jerry, of course. If you live in a town of twenty-five hundred, you know all five of the local cops, and they know you.

I told Jerry that Bunny had shown up at TenHuis Chocolade, and that she said she'd been in the Clown Building the night before. She was sitting with Aunt Nettie and me.

"She doesn't seem to know anything about the— well, the events next door," I said.

"Don't you tell her." Jerry tried to sound stern, but he's too sweet a guy to achieve it.

"And we need Joe," I said. "If you see him, please send him over here."

Jerry assured me that he would.

I went back inside, hoping that my twisted tongue wouldn't let anything slip as I talked to Bunny. I kept looking at my watch as we talked, hoping Joe would show up. But Joe was still missing when Hogan came in, again entering through the alley door.

He looked harassed. "Where is Bunny?"

"In the shop."

"Send her back to the break room. Please."

Bunny obeyed his summons, looking bug-eyed and fearful. She was beginning to see that this interview was important. Hogan served himself a cup of coffee, but Bunny refused one. She just sat down, twisting her hands together.

"Hogan," I said. "Joe is Bunny's lawyer. Maybe she ought to talk to him before she talks to you."

Hogan blinked twice. "That would be fine, if she wants to do that."

Bunny looked amazed. "Why should I need to talk to Joe?"

"As a general rule," I said. "He likes to know what his clients are going to tell the police before they tell it."

"I don't have anything to tell," Bunny said. "Not really. I'd appreciate either you or Mrs. Jones sitting with me while we talk. But we don't need to wait for Joe."

Hogan sighed. "This is just a preliminary session. That would be all right. If you ladies keep quiet."

"Of course," Aunt Nettie said. "We're not lawyers."

"I'm sure I don't know anything," Bunny said.

"Okay," Hogan said. "When did you go over there?"

"Around seven o'clock."

"Why did you go?"

"I wanted to avoid Abigail Birdsong, my husband's aunt. She'd driven up and parked in front of the Ten-Huis Building. I didn't want to talk to her."

"Where were you when you saw her?"

"In the shop. I ducked down behind the counter so she couldn't see me. The lights were off, but she went right up to the window and, you know, held her hands up to look in the window." Bunny demonstrated, forming a tunnel with her hands. "There were lights in the back. I was afraid she'd see me."

Bunny gave a little titter. "I crawled around the

corner and through the door to get to the back room. Then I got up and went through to the Clown Building. I knew she couldn't see me in there."

"What part of that building were you in?"

"You mean the Clown Building?"

Hogan nodded.

"I don't know how to describe it. Near the door. The door from this side into the Clown Building. I guess you'd call it the center."

That would not be near the spot where Abigail's body had been laid out, I realized.

Hogan spoke again. "What did you use for lights?"

"I had a flashlight. But I didn't use it much because I wasn't moving around. There's a chair over there, an old office chair. And a desk. I guess the foreman sits there to write some reports. I sat there." Bunny leaned forward. "But I didn't see anything. Not a body. Nothing."

Hogan didn't reply, and she finally asked the question I'd been wondering about.

"Who was found over there? I mean, whose body?"

I guess Hogan had been waiting for that question, too. There was a long pause before he answered. "It was your aunt."

"My aunt?"

"Yes. Abigail Birdsong. She was found near the back door. Her head was smashed in."

Bunny's jaw dropped.

I imagine that mine did, too. As soon as I got it under control, I spoke. "Then it *was* murder!"

Hogan gave me a warning look.

"Sorry." I murmured the words. "I forgot to shut up."

Bunny hadn't reacted to our exchange. "Someone killed her?"

Hogan nodded.

"Do you know who did it?"

Hogan shook his head.

I was surprised that Bunny didn't burst into tears or otherwise react to the news of Ms. Birdsong's death. She seemed frozen.

"But who would harm Abigail?" Bunny asked.

"You're more likely to know that than I am, Bunny."

"Why?"

"You've lived next door to her for several years." Hogan leaned forward. "I knew Ms. Birdsong only slightly, but I can't imagine her being a distant neighbor."

"Oh no. She wasn't distant."

"Interfering?"

Bunny grimaced. "I'm afraid she was a bit nosy. And full of advice—for me and for Beau."

"For other people, too?

"Mr. Jones—Chief Jones—I'm sure you heard about the big blowup with Anya yesterday afternoon."

"Was that typical?"

"Oh no. It was most unusual. Most people simply let Aunt Abby have her own way. Or at least they didn't argue with her."

"Did you like her, Bunny?"

"We owed her a lot."

"But did you like her?"

Bunny gave a deep sigh. "I guess not. She was so domineering that it was hard to like her."

"Still, hiding in a dark construction site was a pretty drastic way to avoid her."

"I guess so." Bunny's voice sounded quavery.

Hogan opened his mouth, but before he could form it into words, the alley door flew open. We all whirled as Joe came in.

Bunny was the only one of us who spoke. "Oh, Joe! I'm glad to see you. Maybe I should have waited until you came."

Joe's poverty law agency doesn't do criminal law, though he occasionally does a case on his own. He sat down at the table with Hogan and Bunny.

"Sorry," he said. "I didn't mean for you to start without me."

"I don't think I've told the chief anything important," Bunny said defensively.

Joe smiled. "I'm sure it's okay, but I'd still like to talk to you before you say anything more."

"Sure," Hogan said. "I need a break anyway." He got up and headed to our restroom. Joe hoisted Bunny to her feet and walked her up to the retail shop, holding her arm firmly.

"I really didn't see anything, Joe," Bunny said.

"I'm sure you didn't." Joe's voice was soothing.

Aunt Nettie and I sat quietly. I could hear Joe's voice rumble and Bunny's chirp as they talked, but I couldn't understand what they said. Once I heard Bunny speak more loudly—"Oh no!"—and I guessed that Joe had asked her if she was involved in Abigail's death in any way.

I'd know the answer when they came back. If Joe told Bunny not to talk anymore, it would indicate she did know something. If he let her continue talking, she would have denied knowing anything. This is standard procedure in an investigation. I knew that, and Hogan knew more about it than I did, of course.

Anyway, after about five minutes Hogan came back, after about ten Joe and Bunny came back, and nobody asked either Aunt Nettie or me to leave. So I stayed quiet, sitting very still, and so did she.

Hogan asked a few more questions. Bunny said the Clown Building had been empty of people. She'd sat there about ten minutes. No one had come in.

By then, of course, one obvious question was filling my mind. I almost put my hand over my mouth to keep from asking it, but I kept quiet. I'd tell Joe, later. Bunny was his client. He needed to ask the question, not me.

Then Aunt Nettie, who had been almost completely quiet through this entire process, cleared her throat. We all looked at her, and she asked the question I'd been thinking about.

"Excuse me, Bunny, but there's one thing I'd like to know."

"Yes, Mrs. Jones?"

"How did you get into the Clown Building? I mean, it was supposed to be completely locked up."

Chapter 6

Bunny looked completely dismayed. She'd obviously been lying. The only possible alternative was that our security system for the construction project had completely broken down. But I had personally locked that padlock at closing time the night before. I was sure it had been done correctly.

Bunny's mouth formed a big round *O*. Then she whispered, "It should have been locked up, shouldn't it? And I never realized."

There was no answer for her remark, so no one made one. We all sat so quietly that when Joe spoke, Hogan was the only person who didn't jump about a foot.

"Okay," Joe said. "Hogan, are you going to take Bunny downtown?"

Hogan frowned. "It's hard to take anybody 'downtown' in a place the size of Warner Pier."

"In any case, I'm instructing her to stop talking."

"Good enough. If you'll be responsible for keeping her available . . ."

"Of course. I'm sure Bunny intends to stick around in Warner Pier until this matter is straightened out."

Hogan grinned. "I hope she does. Or I could read her her rights."

"That won't be necessary."

Joe escorted Bunny out the front, Hogan left through the back, and Aunt Nettie and I were left looking at each other.

"Did you do that on purpose?" I asked. "Ask that question?"

"I guess so. We've worked so hard on keeping that door locked. For Bunny to act as if it were wide open . . . I sort of saw red."

"Whatever you saw—it's lunchtime. Let's go eat."

We put on our coats and scarves and headed out, winding up at the Sidewalk Café. It's just a block away from TenHuis Chocolade, and it's owned by Joe's step-father, Mike Herrera. It has two other interesting bits of background. First, it's one of the few restaurants in Warner Pier that is open all winter. Second, it's where the tenant of our apartment, Chayslee Brett Zimmerman, is chief chef. I wanted to keep on good terms with Chayslee.

Murder is terribly hard on the relations between a landlord and a tenant. And it's so easy to get a new place to live in Warner Pier in the wintertime.

The Sidewalk Café serves sandwiches, soups, salads, and similar casual fare in a setting that has the theme of sidewalk games. Toys such as roller skates, jump ropes, and jacks decorate the walls; the floors are painted with hopscotch designs.

Small-town lives get entwined. Lindy Herrera, my

best friend since high school and a manager for the restaurant, is married to Tony Herrera, the son of the owner of the restaurant, Mike Herrera. Mike Herrera had married Joe's mom a couple of years earlier. Joe and Tony were stars of the wrestling team in high school, and they're still best buddies. If we drew a diagram of our relationships, it would look like some backwoods family in which cousins marry cousins.

Lindy was on duty that day, seating patrons. Our arrival followed the lunch rush, which is minimal in the winter, of course. Since the restaurant wasn't too busy, I told Lindy we'd like to talk to Chayslee.

"That is, if she has a minute," I said. "We can wait for her, if we're not occupying a table you need."

"I'll stick you in the corner," Lindy said. "Stay as long as you like. Chayslee should have time to talk to you before long. Plus, I want to know just what was happening at your place this morning. Is it true that Abigail Birdsong was found dead?"

So we gave Lindy a personal report. She listened with wide eyes, complete with the comments I was sure everyone was making: "It's hard to believe it's Abigail Birdsong!" and "Does Hogan have any idea who did it?"

The Warner Pier gossip was in full battle cry, and I knew Lindy would be adding ammunition.

We ordered—French dip for me and chicken salad and vegetable soup for Aunt Nettie—and in around fifteen minutes Chef Chayslee delivered our orders personally, then sat down with us.

Chayslee is an attractive gal who I'd guess is in her late twenties. She has blond hair, worn up in a bun for work, and clear blue eyes. Despite working with food all day, she's slender, and she always seems peppy.

"I'm caught up for a minute," she said. "What was going on over at TenHuis this morning?"

"I hoped the police had told you," I said. "I hate to break the news that we had a murder last night. The body was found right under your apartment."

"That's what I heard. What happened?"

Aunt Nettie and I quickly sketched the story we'd gotten from Hogan. I ended with an offer. "If you feel nervous about staying in your apartment after this, Joe and I have a guest room with bath available. You can stay with us until they figure out what's going on."

Then I panicked. Joe might have already asked Bunny to stay. That's the kind of thing he's apt to do. "I mean, I'd have to check. But we can find you a place where you'll feel safari."

Chayslee blinked, and I realized my tongue had twisted into a knot. "I mean safe!" I yelped. "We want you to feel safe. And happy."

"Happy?" Chayslee sounded surprised.

Aunt Nettie, ever tactful, saved the day. "Good tenants are valuable," she said. "In a resort area, people come and go all the time. We treasure you, Chayslee."

Chayslee laughed. "I treasure having a newly decorated apartment a block from my job, with plumbing that works and a responsive landlord. So don't worry. I'm not going anyplace for a while. I have only one problem, and that one's minor."

Aunt Nettie perked her ears up like a terrier, and I'm sure I did, too. We spoke in unison. "A problem?"

Chayslee laughed. "Oh, it's just the cats. Or I guess that's what it is."

"Cats?" I probably sounded incredulous, and Aunt Nettie's voice was horrified. "We can't have animals of any kind around a food service business," she said.

"Oh, they're not *in* the building," Chayslee said. "It must be feral cats of some sort. They raise a commotion in the Dumpsters now and then. I first began to notice it a couple of weeks ago."

A commotion near the Dumpsters? We'd never heard any mention of that before. And where would feral cats come from? Of course, stray cats can turn up anyplace, but they certainly weren't usual in downtown Warner Pier.

"I'll ask Dolly if she's heard them," I said. "But back to today's problem—have you talked to the detectives yet?"

"No. One of them came up here and asked me to be available after work."

"Better mention the cats, Chayslee."

"If you think so." She shrugged and went back to work. Aunt Nettie and I ate our lunches, then headed to the shop. As soon as I was at my desk, I called Dolly Jolly, Aunt Nettie's chief assistant.

I had planned to ask Dolly about the cats, but there was no answer either in her apartment or on her cell phone. I left a message.

"Why are you so interested in those cats?" Aunt Nettie asked.

"It just seems odd. We've never seen or heard cats in the alley. The Dumpster lid is tightly closed, and we keep trash picked up around them."

"I'm sure Hogan's crew checked the Dumpsters all up and down the alley."

"I'm sure you're right. Plus, we don't see any other kind of animal who might be interested in Dumpsters in downtown alleys here in Warner Pier."

"But we do see stray cats, Lee. Sometimes."

"True. And I even find that hard to believe. Maybe it's the Texan in me coming out. I can't imagine a cat out in the nights we have around here. You'd think we'd find them stiff as boards if they didn't have shelter."

Aunt Nettie laughed indulgently. As a Warner Pier native, she finds my awe of Michigan's cold winters amusing. But I certainly wouldn't want any cat I knew out in below-twenty-degree temperatures.

I also left a message for Joe, but got no reply. I tried to catch up on some work, in case Bunny showed up Monday, ready to be trained for her new job. The likelihood of her starting Monday wasn't strong, I realized. She'd probably be down at the police department, facing questions about her aunt Abigail. But I needed to ask Joe if I could repeat my invitation to Chayslee.

I also called Dolly Jolly once more, and this time she answered.

"Hi, Lee. I went over to see my mom last night and drove home after lunch today!" she shouted. "I just now noticed the message light is flashing! What's up?"

"Have you heard cats in the alley?"

"Cats? You mean, 'meow, meow' cats?"

I laughed. "They might be 'purr, purr' cats. Anyway, some sort of animals around the Dumpster."

"No. But, Lee, remember how my apartment's laid out? The kitchen and bath are in the middle, the living room at the back, and the bedroom in front! I don't ever hear a lot from the alley, once I get in bed! But sometimes people or animals on the street keep me awake!"

I repeated Chayslee's story. "I told her she ought to tell the police."

"What for?"

I realized that Dolly had been gone the previous night. She wouldn't know anything about the murder.

So I told her. The news of Abigail's death seemed to

be all over town, so I ignored Hogan's previous instructions.

By the time Dolly and I had hashed over the whole story, it was quitting time. Not that I'd gotten any work done during an entire day at the office. Janie had come in to work, but I had sent her home. No one would come through that yellow tape. It was a wasted day as far as business went.

I offered Dolly a bed for the night, but like Chayslee, she declined.

I was nearly out the door when Joe finally called. He sounded harassed. "Hey. What's up?"

I quickly sketched my invitations to Chayslee and Dolly.

Joe chuckled. "You're getting as bad as I am," he said.

"We're both caring people who worry about others."

He chuckled more loudly. "Or complete busybodies. I haven't figured out which."

"Or maybe both. Anyway, Dolly has declined, and Chayslee was indefinite but leaning toward no. May I repeat the invitation to her?"

"As far as I'm concerned. Maybe she'll cook dinner."

"That sounds good. If you rely on me, it's bacon and eggs. How did things go with Bunny?"

"She's staying in the room she rents from Clara Vanderberg."

"Clara didn't throw her out?"

"Clara's so wild to know what's going on that she even invited Bunny to dinner. And Bunny and I have an appointment with Hogan at nine a.m. tomorrow."

"Is Bunny's story sounding better?"

Joe sighed deeply, and there was a long pause.

I spoke. "It can't already be time for a plea bargain."

"No." Joe's voice lacked conviction.

"You don't believe her," I said.

"Well. It's just that . . ."

"Oh, spit it out, Joe! What's she saying now?"

Joe gave another sigh. "Lee, she's still telling the same story."

"The same story?"

"Right. She still swears that the door between the two buildings was not locked. And she doesn't remember a thing about the padlock. In her story, it wasn't even there."

Chapter 7

Bunny was sticking to her story?

I had no answer to that remark. Or maybe I had questions, too many questions. Such as, how could Bunny stick to a statement that was obviously not true? Or how could she hope to convince Hogan that the door I had carefully padlocked was later standing wide open? Even though the key was locked in a drawer in my desk? Or how could she answer a million other questions?

I didn't argue when Joe said he'd see me at home. We both hung up.

I called Chayslee's cell phone—by now she was home—and she said she had talked to Hogan, giving her statement, and she'd been assured that law enforcement would be on the scene all night. So she was declining our invitation, though she did appreciate it.

Everybody seemed to be taken care of, so I headed home. Joe was there before I was—he'd apparently made any phone calls he needed to make before he called me. He lit a fire he'd laid earlier, and we each indulged in a bottle of Labatt Blue and some crackers and cheese.

It had sure been a strange day. I didn't feel a lot of grief for Abigail Birdsong, of course. I'd only met the woman the previous afternoon, and I'd found her quite obnoxious. I was sorry for what had happened to her, but it wasn't personal. It almost gave me a sense of relief. Now she wouldn't be bugging poor Bunny, and maybe Hogan would discover the guilty person had nothing to do with Bunny, and maybe . . . Well, maybe a lot of things would happen, and I hoped none of them would prolong Bunny's problems.

Ha.

I sat next to Joe on the couch and stared at the fire. "Okay, Joe," I said. "Can you share Bunny's full story?"

"I guess so. She's going to tell it to Hogan tomorrow morning."

"So? What the heck was she doing in the Clown Building last night?"

"Just what she said. She was hiding from Abigail Birdsong."

"Sitting in the pitch-dark, in an unheated building. Maybe with a body laid out within a few feet of her."

"Bunny still swears that Abigail was in the street outside, banging on the front door. She's sure the body wasn't there."

"I hope it wasn't. This story is weird enough without adding that detail. And don't forget the padlock on the door between the two buildings. I'm sure I locked up before I left. So how could Bunny get into the TenHuis Building, let alone the Clown Building?"

"Apparently Dolly let her into the TenHuis shop."

"Dolly? Why? When?"

"I haven't talked to Dolly. She's not my client. But Bunny says she snuck out of work early, trying to avoid a quarrel with her soon-to-be ex-husband. So she thought she should come back and finish up her work. Bunny apparently went up to Dolly's apartment, got the keys from her, and went in through the street door. She turned on some lights, of course. She says she was straightening a new office. Then Abigail came to the front window, and Bunny thought she was looking for her, for Bunny. Bunny didn't want to talk to Abigail. So she hid."

"I wonder if Dolly heard anything. I mean, from her apartment upstairs. No, that won't work. Dolly went to see her mom."

"Apparently she was leaving just as Bunny stopped by. But the question I'm most interested in isn't for Dolly."

"Who is it for, then?"

"I'm not sure."

"And what is this question?"

"It's a simple one. The question is, what if Bunny's story is true? What if the padlock wasn't locked? What if there was no lock between the TenHuis Building and the Clown Building? Who unlocked it?"

Joe was right. It definitely put a different complexion on the whole crime.

I thought a moment. "How about the murder weapon? Has Hogan told you what that was?"

"He's told me it could be a lot of things. Which means they don't know yet. Maybe the scientific crew will come up with something."

"It's more likely Hogan will have to find a blunt

instrument, and then the crew will consider it," I said. "But I have another question."

"And it is?"

"Why the heck would anyone want into that building anyway? There's nothing much there. The workmen leave a few tools overnight. Did the killer want to steal a hammer or a screwdriver?"

"The killer might have wanted to get in purely and simply because he wanted to get a dead body off the street."

A rabbit ran over my grave, and I shuddered. "Using our building as an impromptu graveyard? What a horrible idea, Joe."

"It does seem as if it would have been easier to toss the evidence in the Dumpster."

"Evidence as large as a body isn't too easy to toss around."

Joe smiled at me. "Maybe we'd better think about something more cheerful. Do you want to go out to dinner?"

We decided to settle for bacon and eggs at home, as I'd mentioned earlier. A piece of rye toast with an omelet improved my mood, but it didn't do anything to answer the questions Joe and I had raised.

In fact, I came up with more questions. I'd been assuming, in my simpleminded way, that someone killed Abigail Birdsong simply because she was an obnoxious woman who liked her own way. But there are hundreds of obnoxious women around. Only rarely do they get murdered. Did the police have any ideas of a motive?

Joe hadn't heard anything.

Love or money? Those are the usual motives. Was one of those involved?

But love didn't seem to be a likely motive for anyone to kill Abigail. She was a plain, tough-spoken, managing older woman. Of course, that didn't mean someone might not fall in love with her. Someone, or even two someones, might have a grand passion for plain, tough-spoken, managing elderly women. Stranger things have happened.

But money certainly seemed a more likely motive than love. And Abigail, I reminded myself, had just that afternoon threatened to change her will.

That put Bunny even deeper in trouble, since Abigail had stated firmly that she planned to cut Beau out and make Bunny her main heir.

Or did it? If Bunny was a potential heir, wouldn't she make sure the new will had been signed before she got rid of Aunt Abigail?

I finally got in bed and turned on the dumbest television program I could find. I needed to forget. I fell asleep immediately.

The next morning was Sunday, and I was prepared to sleep late. Until the phone rang.

"Hello." My voice was weak.

"Lee!" Dolly's voice was strong.

I propped the phone on my ear. "Dolly? What's up?"

"Do cops ever sleep?"

"I'm sure they do. Sometime." I didn't move anything but my mouth. "Why do you need to know?"

"Your uncle called! He wants to come by and interview me! Now! And I'm barely out of bed."

"That's logical, Dolly. I imagine that he simply needs something confirmed."

Such as the things Bunny had told him, I thought. I didn't say anything; Hogan might want to talk to Dolly about a completely different topic.

Dolly made noises about hanging up, but I stopped her. "Hey, Dolly! Wait a minute. Did you hear any cats in the alley last night?"

"I didn't hear one!" Dolly hung up.

No cats in the Dumpster. Hmmm. But, of course, there were police there. Supposedly. It would probably be a single cop, in a patrol car. One cop couldn't be everyplace all the time.

I roused myself slowly. It was Sunday. My day off, supposedly. But could Sunday be a day off when I took Saturday off? Did I need to catch up?

But the reason I needed to catch up was so that I could have Monday to train Bunny.

But would Bunny be there to be trained on Monday? Or would she be in the hoosegow?

I sat up and held my head in my hands. Joe was already in the shower. The clock said seven o'clock. He and Bunny had an appointment with Hogan at nine.

Oh heck! At least I could fix Joe a decent breakfast. I got up, ground coffee, and began to make pancakes.

By eight forty-five Joe left to meet Bunny and Hogan. By nine forty-five I'd had my shower and was headed for TenHuis Chocolade.

The advantage of working at a time your business is supposed to be closed, of course, is that few people phone, and you can ignore the ones who do. I was really turning out the work when I heard Dolly come in the alley door. I kept my head ducked. I couldn't think of any particular business reason she would need to talk to me, and I didn't want to be disturbed for any other reason that morning.

That didn't stop Dolly, of course. She came blasting through the workroom, shouting my name. "Hey, Lee!"

I kept my head down and waved. Dolly could see

me through the glass walls of my office, but I didn't answer her.

Dolly stopped in the door of my office. "Lee, I got a funny idea from talking to Hogan this morning!"

"Funny ha-ha? Or funny peculiar?"

"Funny peculiar, I guess!"

"Why not? Everything else is funny peculiar. What did Hogan ask you?"

"Oh, a lot of stuff about who locks up, who opens up? Stuff like that!"

"That doesn't seem too peculiar."

"But, Lee, I think he's going to want to search our building! The TenHuis Building."

Chapter 8

Why not?

If you looked at it from Hogan's point of view, he should have had our building searched as soon as Abigail Birdsong's body was found. Our building connected with the crime scene. It was amazing that Hogan and/or the state police detectives hadn't had the floorboards up, searching for knives, guns, and clubs before Abigail Birdsong was carried away for an autopsy.

Actually I remembered Hogan coming through our office, looking around casually, and asking a few questions. But he hadn't searched, not Searched with a capital S.

I decided the detectives simply hadn't had time to search the day before. Our building hadn't been a priority.

So I grinned at Dolly. "I guess Hogan's hints have

given us time to hide anything incriminating. But for now I'm working as usual."

Dolly went on her way, and I tried to get some letters out of the way. About an hour later Aunt Nettie came bustling in and told me Hogan had officially asked her for permission to search the premises of TenHuis Chocolade.

"Of course, I said it would be fine," she said.

I chuckled, as I had with Dolly. "After all the favors Hogan and his crew have done for us, we can hardly refuse to cooperate with them. When do they want to come?"

"This afternoon."

"Sunday afternoon's probably the least disruptive time, since we're closed then this time of the year."

"I'm sure they won't find anything."

"I'm sure there's nothing to find. After all, the crime happened next door to us. Not in our building."

Aunt Nettie nodded enthusiastically.

"Whenever they show up," I said, "I'll get out of the way."

I did stop with my fingers poised over the keyboard and worry for a moment. Hogan had also been scheduled to meet with Bunny and Joe that morning. How had that gone?

I shrugged. I knew of nothing I could do to find out. Joe was completely immersed in Bunny's problems. When he had something he was willing to share with me, he would. Forget it, I told myself.

The state police crew showed up at noon. I turned them over to Aunt Nettie and went down to the Sidewalk Café, telling her to call me when the search was over.

I was eating a bowl of vegetable soup and playing

a game on my cell phone when the phone rang. It was
Aunt Nettie. Her voice sounded shaky.

"What's wrong?" I asked.

Aunt Nettie gave a weak little laugh. "Why do you
ask that?"

"Because your voice sounds as if you're upset. Did
the state police find anything?"

"Maybe. But I guess you'd better come down here.
The stairway . . . Well, I need you, Lee."

The stairway? Did TenHuis Chocolade even have a
stairway?

I thought frantically as I paid for my soup, put on
my jacket, and headed toward my office. By then I was
thinking straighter, and I'd remembered that the Ten-
Huis Building did have a stairway. It had two. One led
to the basement. The other was simply not something
Aunt Nettie and I considered part of the business, so
I'd buried all references to it someplace in my subconscious. I'd forgotten its existence completely.

The layouts of our building and of the Clown Building were so routine to Warner Pier that I had forgotten
that most of them had a second set of stairs.

We Warner Pierites are proud of our cute, picturesque downtown, and we advertise it everyplace. We
have narrow streets, laid out in the 1850s, and the business district is entirely made up of two-story redbrick
buildings. Nearly all of them were constructed in between 1890 and 1920. They've been updated occasionally over their more than a hundred years of existence,
and now nearly every one of them has large plate glass
show windows.

Some have been deliberately made more picturesque than others, and some are more modern-looking

than the city fathers would prefer. But they're pretty uniform.

Most of our buildings have twenty-five-foot fronts, though some owners have thrown two buildings together and have fifty-foot fronts. This is how TenHuis Chocolade and the Clown Building were to come out, once they were joined together. The typical Warner Pier building has a narrow front door in the center, with a show window on either side.

The second story of each building is brick, with ordinary double-hung windows at regular intervals. Any woodwork, on either the first floor or the second, is painted white. The buildings usually extend seventy-five feet from front to back.

As I've said, nearly every building in downtown Warner Pier has an apartment over it. And at either the front or the back of each building, there's a stairway that leads from the outside—either the street or the alley—to the apartment.

In the case of both the TenHuis Building and the Clown Building, there is a stairway at both the front end and the back end of the structure. And in front of each building a small, inconspicuous doorway opens onto the street.

Dolly Jolly lived over our building, and Chayslee Zimmerman lived over the Clown Building. For ordinary use, both Dolly and Chayslee and their guests go up and down those front stairs. On the street each staircase has a solid door with a solid lock. The stairs inside are steep and lead straight up to a door at the top, a door that comes out in the center of the building. That door is also kept locked—or I suppose it is. That would be up to the tenant, but most people today keep their front doors locked, wherever they live.

Both the buildings have another little quirk.

They were built when business proprietors found it convenient to live over their businesses. That was the original purpose of each of the apartments. They weren't built as rentals for summer residents. They were there to provide housing for business owners or managers.

As a result, each had a back entrance that led directly down to the business underneath. In the cases of our building and the Clown Building, neither tenant used that entrance routinely. But it was there. They could use it if they wished.

The back stairway from each apartment led down to an alley door. At the alley door there was a small room that could be called a foyer. It was about five feet square and had one door that led to the alley and one that led into the main business premises.

The doors were rarely used, of course. After all, what tenant wants to enter her home through a small door on a dark alley when she can go in and out through a well-lighted door on a main business street?

But this plan meant Dolly's apartment had a back stairway I'd forgotten existed. Because TenHuis Chocolade had a different alley door. Ours exited from our break room. No one used the original back way to and from the apartment stairs. Oh, at one time Dolly had used it, when she parked in a garage across the alley. But it hadn't been used for quite a while.

By the time I'd finished this analysis, I was at TenHuis. I rapped at the street door, and a uniformed state police officer opened it for me. I could see Aunt Nettie at the back of the building. The rarely used back door to Dolly's back stairs was standing open, and a bright light was shining inside.

Aunt Nettie seemed to be wringing her hands. I sped back to the break room and gave her a hug.

"Oh, Lee!" she said. "I hadn't looked into that stairwell for years."

She was so upset that I was afraid to look in it myself. I let go of her, took three deep breaths, and leaned over to get a better view inside the stairwell.

By then I expected to see a body sprawled on the stairs. But I didn't see that.

I didn't see anything for a long moment. The bright light seemed to blind me, so I stood there and blinked.

Then I saw the stains on the stairs.

I'm no authority on stains, but it looked like blood to me.

I again took three deep breaths. "Come on, Auntie," I said. "Let's sit down."

"Oh, Lee, when I think of that poor woman, lying there . . ."

Now Hogan was on the other side of her. "Now, Nettie, I don't think she was there very long. And she was probably already dead."

Hogan's efforts, of course, were much more soothing than mine. Pretty soon Aunt Nettie calmed down to her usual placid attitude.

"Well, at least they moved her next door," she said. "No telling how long Abigail Birdsong would have been there if she'd been left on the stairway."

Aunt Nettie had already explained how rarely the door was used, either by the shop or by Dolly. Hogan and the top state police detective were now hashing over the situation. I sat and listened, but I finally spoke.

"But finding the blood in the stairway has compounded the problem," I said.

Hogan nodded, and the state detective frowned.

"Right," Hogan said. "It confuses the matter of how the perpetrators got into your building. Now they had to have two keys, not just one."

Yes, we now knew that whoever had neatly laid out Abigail Birdsong had needed to get into our building, then open the door between the buildings—the one with the strong padlock—and carry Abigail's body into the other building.

Now, with the discovery of the blood on the unused stairway, it was plain that they had also needed to get into that back entrance to Dolly's apartment and either kill Abigail there or store her body there temporarily. An extra key for the door to the back stairway would have been required.

Hogan had obviously been thinking along the same lines. "So, Lee," he said, "are you the keeper of the keys?"

For a moment I couldn't even remember. Then I pictured a tangle of keys and key chains.

"They're in my desk," I said. "And they're in a real mess."

I led Hogan and Aunt Nettie up to the office, took my desk key from my purse, and opened the left-hand bottom drawer. I reached toward the box that held the keys, but Hogan stopped me.

"Maybe we'd better do a little fingerprinting," he said.

So Aunt Nettie and I went back to the break room and watched detectives and technicians dig in drawers and look behind furniture. Up front in my office, we could see the same sort of action going on.

"I'm almost sorry for those techs," I said. "I'm not even sure all of those keys have labels."

"I wonder if they've realized that Dolly probably has keys, too," Aunt Nettie said.

"And I wonder if they realize that some of those keys have fingerprints on them that are from people who are no longer here."

I was sure one set of keys had belonged to Hazel TerHoot, who had been Aunt Nettie's chief assistant until she retired two years earlier.

"Where is Dolly?" Aunt Nettie asked.

"This is Dolly's day off," I said. "I'm sure the state police are looking for her."

"She supposedly gave keys to Bunny."

"That would have been a different set," I said. "Probably Dolly's own keys. But I know she has an extra key to her apartment she keeps upstairs."

Aunt Nettie gave a deep sigh, and the two of us sat for twenty minutes or so. Waiting. Then Hogan and the state police detective came back. Hogan was carrying a dozen or so small paper bags. They rattled when he moved them.

"We need you to ID these," he said.

He started to spread out a newspaper, but Aunt Nettie offered him a dish towel in its place. When that was laid neatly on the break room table, he adjusted his rubber gloves, removed the keys from their sacks, and laid them on the towel.

The keys looked pretty routine. Most of them were plain keys with small tags tied to them with string. Hogan gave me rubber gloves, and I picked each key up.

"Back door," the first tag read. The others had similarly informative titles. I read the tag of one with three keys: "'My desk. Duplicate for mail box. Extra front/back door.' Actually, Aunt Nettie has a duplicate set of these in her desk."

Aunt Nettie frowned. "I try to remember to keep

them locked up, but it's possible some people know where they are. I mean, someone might need them."

I was pawing among the tags with one rubber-gloved finger. "Yes, we had those three made for Dolly when she first came. Later we gave her a full set, and she used the Raggedy Ann set as a backup."

I picked up the keys and eyed the inch-high charm attached to the key chain. The charm was an enamel version of a famous doll from history. "Yes, it's Raggedy Ann. Dolly's doll. Dolly said her sister gave it to her."

"These must be the keys Dolly gave Bunny," Hogan said. "We'll have to ask Bunny what she did with them after she left TenHuis that night."

He didn't say anything more, but the answer to that question quivered in the air. Why would Bunny put the keys into my drawer, rather than giving them directly back to Dolly? Of course, she could leave the building without keys; she just couldn't get back inside without them.

The mystery of the keys had deepened with questions about Bunny. But whatever the answers were, the questions made Bunny look more and more guilty.

Who's Who in Chocolate

MONTEZUMA

Montezuma was the Aztec emperor who had to face the invading Spanish in the 1500s. But the two civilizations had many chances to observe each other before their final confrontation, in which Montezuma died.

The Spanish were fascinated with this new—to them—civilization, of course. All sorts of legends have developed about the Aztecs and their ruler.

One is that he drank chocolate as an aphrodisiac before visiting his harem, having as much as fifty large jars of cocoa. And, so *they* say, he had hundreds of wives. But only two queens. To a nonhistorian such as JoAnna Carl, this sounds as if a lot of brides were presented to the emperor as a matter of state, perhaps similar to events in the Old Testament.

Historians also take the aphrodisiac tale with a grain of (Spanish) salt, since Montezuma didn't leave written records, and the Spanish did. The invaders may have been having physical problems due to their diet of nothing but meat, and may have been the ones looking for a pick-me-up for all their bodily functions.

Chapter 9

Soon after that the search was finished, and Aunt Nettie and I both went home. I was feeling really down, deeply worried about Bunny.

At home I found Joe's truck in its parking spot, and Joe himself waiting in the kitchen.

"I talked Bunny into staying for a night or two," he said. "She's in the south bedroom. I hope that's all right."

"Sure. But things don't look good for her, Joe."

Keeping my voice low, I quickly ran over the results of the search of TenHuis Chocolade, at least as far as I knew them. When I got to the part about the blood-stains in the rarely used stairwell, Joe whistled.

"Bunny admits she saw Abigail through the window," I said. "And she had access to the keys. Frankly, I wouldn't be surprised if Hogan showed up here this evening with an arrest warrant. I'm almost surprised they haven't issued one already."

"Instead of coming out and arresting her, Hogan

would probably ask Bunny to turn herself in," he said. "There are a lot of unanswered questions still."

"Did Bunny tell you anything new today?"

"Not really. She still says that the door between the buildings was standing open. She says Dolly gave her her own keys and told her to leave them in the office."

"But I'm still surprised that there's no warrant out."

"One reason they won't arrest her—yet—is that they have no motive. And I convinced them Bunny was unlikely to simply go berserk and kill an aunt-in-law."

"No motive?" I thought about it carefully. "I guess you're right. I suppose that I was thinking about Abigail's threat to change her will and leave her entire estate to Bunny. That would definitely be a motive."

"But not for Bunny. That would be a motive for Beau. Abigail hadn't had time to do anything about her will. So it was to Bunny's advantage to keep Abigail alive."

A load lifted from my tiny brain. "Whew!" I said. "I knew that, but hearing you say it makes me feel better."

"It doesn't make me feel much better," Joe said. "But I've got to hang on to something, so I'll grab hold of that idea."

I went upstairs to talk to Bunny, clinging to that information all the way up.

Of course, I told myself. Abigail had been in my office as late as four o'clock on Friday, headed for Holland. I had surmised that she was going to make a new will.

If someone told me about a lawyer who agreed to turn out a will after four o'clock on a Friday, I'd find a bridge I could sell them. Lawyers usually don't work that late. Certainly their clerical staff doesn't want to. Abigail simply hadn't had time to change her will before she died.

I ignored the likelihood that Abigail might have

been a very important client, one a lawyer might stay late for. If that were true, Hogan would have already tracked that lawyer down.

Besides, when it came to the will, I had thought that Abigail had announced her plan to change her will mainly as a threat. She wanted to whip Beau into line, not disinherit him. She might well make the new will, then never sign it.

Upstairs I greeted Bunny and assured her that she was welcome to stay. After making sure she had towels, soap, and other things guests need, I went downstairs, ready to cook dinner. I had stopped for ground beef on the way home, and I dug out macaroni, onions, tomato sauce, and other stuff. It would serve to make that immortal American dish Joe calls goulash, even though no Hungarian ever saw anything like it. In my family it was known as Mom's Quick Hamburger Skillet Mess. That and a salad would get us to the table fast. I'd pull out some misdecorated Strawberry Cheesecake truffles ("white chocolate ganache enrobed with dark or white chocolate and embellished with pink and white chocolate stripes"—only these had milk chocolate stripes). We'd be eating in forty-five minutes.

Why the rush? To be honest, mostly because of the discovery of Dolly's keys, I felt we had to eat in a hurry. Maybe we could get the dishes done before Bunny was arrested.

But she wasn't arrested. Not that night.

The next morning was Monday, and all three of us got up and got ready for work, pretending to be normal people. At breakfast Joe told Bunny he'd talk to Hogan, then report anything he found out.

When I looked questioning, he mouthed the name "Dolly." Apparently he meant that he expected Hogan to question Dolly before he came back for another round with Bunny.

So I drove Bunny by the house where she was living, and dropped her off to change clothes before she went to work. Then I drove by the post office, parked, and went inside, my usual way to begin the working day.

And there was Beau.

He was his usual beautiful self—long, pale blond ponytail shining in the winter sun, handsome, tall, a regular sun god. He made me want to upchuck.

I was extremely angry with Beau, which led me to do something tacky. I stopped and spoke to him.

"Hi, Beau."

Beau turned toward me with a gracious bow. "Hello, Lee."

"I'm terribly worried about Bunny. Are you going to be able to do something to help her?"

"Bunny? Help Bunny? Why?"

"She certainly seems to need help."

"What for?" Then he gave a little gasp. "You haven't had to fire her, have you?"

"No."

"Thank God. She's so incompetent."

"I was talking about her legal problems."

"The divorce? Why should she need help with that?"

The clouds were beginning to clear for me, and I was starting to catch on. Beau apparently knew nothing about the murder of his aunt.

I gave a short sniff. "Beau, haven't you heard about Bunny's new problems?"

"What problems?"

I didn't answer, and for the first time I realized we had the attention of the entire post office. Since it was the time of the morning when about 80 percent of the town's businesspeople emptied their boxes, that was a sizable portion of the Warner Pier population.

Beau was still frowning at me, his eyebrows knitting hard enough to produce a pair of mittens.

"Beau," I said, "I'd better shut up, but I feel sure the police are looking for a statement from you."

"From me? What is it? What's happened? Is something wrong?"

I kept quiet. And to my surprise, so did everyone else in the post office. I walked away. In a minute Beau dropped out of the line and skedaddled out of the post office and down Peach Street.

And I saw expressions of satisfaction on every face in the room.

I hadn't realized how disliked Beau had become. Now I realized that public opinion was firmly on Bunny's side. By divorcing the meek little thing, he had—well, we Texans would say he had shot himself in the foot. Maybe we Michiganders would say the same thing.

I grabbed envelopes from the PO box, stood in line for a package, then put my mail in a tote bag I carried in the van for that purpose. I headed to the office, where Janie told me Joe was there and talking to Bunny. So I headed to the little office in the back.

There I found Joe busy with a measuring tape and Bunny behind her desk picking up paper clips from the floor. Apparently she'd dropped a box of two hundred back there.

"What on earth are you up to?" I asked Joe.

"I was wondering if we could put a small door between your offices, so that you and Bunny could communicate face-to-face, instead of sending e-mails and text messages through this wall."

"Ahem," I said. "I'm sure you recall that—once we

get the other building in operation—this whole area
will be expanded into a real office. There will be room
for two more clerical workers, as yet not hired, and
even an office for Aunt Nettie."

"Still, that will be several months, Lee. And I could
come down one night this week and put a door in right
here. Easy."

"No. Bunny and I will just run down the hall to see
each other. Or use the intercom. Or, I'll bang on the wall."

Joe's face fell. He loves a good construction project.
"Oh well," he said.

Then he grinned. "Anyway, Hogan says he's got to
question a lot more people about Abigail Birdsong's
death before he has any more questions for Bunny. So
let's try not to worry today."

"Okay, Mr. Cheery," I said. "Whom does he have to
question?"

"Dolly, for one. Apparently she got back from her
mother's Saturday afternoon, then left her apartment
early yesterday afternoon, and hasn't been seen since."

"I noticed she wasn't around."

"Right. Also missing are Beau, along with Anya and
Andrew Hartley. The three of them apparently went
someplace late Friday or early Saturday, and they
haven't shown up since. I don't know if they've flown
the coop . . ."

"Oh no!" Bunny's voice was distressed. "Beau
would never run away!"

"Maybe not, but he needs to make a statement. Plus,
as Mrs. Birdsong's closest relative, he needs to take
charge of the funeral plans. And he hasn't shown up
to assume that duty."

"Beau is back from wherever he went," I said. I described the scene in the post office, ending with, "I

gather Beau isn't the most popular guy in town just at the moment."

"Poor Beau," Bunny said.

I thought I caught an echo of pity in her voice.

The woman was unbelievable. How could she feel pity for a rat like Beau?

"I guess I should call Hogan and let him know Beau is around," I said.

Bunny spoke again. "As soon as I realized that he wasn't in town, I called and left a message on the answering machine at the house."

Bunny was still taking care of her ex, the most undeserving jerk in Michigan.

I told Joe to go away and do whatever he needed to do. Then I sat down to explain Bunny's new job to her. I started with the form for the e-mail orders. A large majority of our orders come in that way. And you'd be surprised how many of them need a confirming phone call or message before the order can go back to be shipped.

We worked at that for a couple of hours, and I was very pleased at how quickly Bunny caught on to the whole thing. During this session, her pencil rolled off the table four times, she ran her office chair over her toe once, and she knocked her coffee cup over twice. Luckily it had a tight lid. She was still our accidental Bunny, clumsy as ever.

After that session Bunny went for an early lunch, and I went to my own desk and started sorting the mail.

Three envelopes, I was sure, held orders for Easter items. I put those aside for Bunny to handle. Another was an order for wedding favors. I recognized the return address of the bride. I'd handle those. In the remaining stack I had a letter from the Michigan State Chamber of Commerce, telling me about a workshop they planned; a begging letter from my alma mater, the University of Texas–Dallas; and similar letters from a health research organization, a museum, and an arts organization. I put all those in their proper place and then picked up the final envelope.

It was plain white, the kind sold nearly anyplace. It was hand addressed to me at the TenHuis street address, not at our PO box. So it was lucky I got it.

And the return address read, "Abigail Birdsong, 112 W. Lakeside, Warner Pier, MI." It ended with the zip.

I stared at it dully for a moment. Then I stood up. I think I intended to yell, but I was so startled that I whispered.

"Oh! My! Gosh!"

I was extremely tempted to rip it open. What had Abigail Birdsong sent me?

But I behaved as a proper citizen should and called Hogan. He'd need to examine it for fingerprints and other evidence when it was opened.

After my call, Hogan took no more than five minutes to show up and take the letter back to the police department for scientific examination. I went along, and I paced the floor until he could allow me to see the mysterious missive.

When Hogan finally opened it, wearing rubber gloves, its pages were covered with small, tight handwriting. But the first paragraph gave the whole thing away.

"Last will and testimony of Abigail Joan Birdsong," it read.

When I saw it, I yelped. "Oh, ye gods! But why'd she send it to me?"

Chapter 10

Of course, I should have been a good little citizen of Michigan and allowed the authorities to take a look at the document first. But I was only slightly good. Hogan dropped the will flat on a desk, and we looked at it together.

But I kept talking. "Hogan, does Michigan even recognize holographic wills?"

"They sure do, Lee. Of course, we'd have to prove it was in Abigail's handwriting and that she actually made it. But it ought to be okay."

The will did just what it was supposed to do. It stated what Abigail Birdsong wanted done with her property. It didn't list the property or go into a lot of details. It named a lawyer as executor.

There was a decided tone of "that'll show 'em" to the document. "Because of her kindness to me over a number of years" was one phrase. "Specifically excluding closer relatives" was another.

And the will did what Abigail had threatened. It left everything to Barbara Jane Culpepper Birdsong, "also known as Bunny Birdsong."

The will was only one page long. In addition to Abigail Birdsong's signature, at the bottom two more people had signed as witnesses: Felix Perez and Elizabeth Ray.

I pointed to the names. "Aren't those two on the staff at the Sidewalk Café?"

"I believe so," Hogan said. "We'll check to make sure Abigail ate dinner there. If she did, they would be logical witnesses."

The will had been written on ordinary, cheap, yellow, lined paper, the kind usually called a "legal pad." Those pads are sold nearly everywhere. I knew there was a display of stationery items at the Downtown Drugstore, and I was sure it would include a tablet such as this one. The sheet of paper had been folded and mailed in an envelope that also might have come from that same display.

Attached to the will, near the top, was a Post-it note. Its yellow was so close to the color of the tablet that I hadn't seen it at first. The note on it was in the same cramped handwriting as the will.

"Mrs. Woodyard," it read. "Please put this into the proper hands, either Bunny's or your husband's, since I believe he is Bunny's legal representative. Abigail Birdsong."

"Huh," I said. "Bunny's going to be a wealthy woman, if Abigail's financial reputation is based on fact. But Bunny's so meek! There's not a chance in the world that she can hold on to the money."

"She may not even get it," Hogan said.

"Why not? You said a holographic will is legal in the state of Michigan."

"It is. But this particular will sure gives Bunny something else she hasn't had: a motive. And if she's convicted of killing Abigail, she's not going to get a cent."

That pricked my balloon. I could feel myself deflate.

"Means, motive, and opportunity," Hogan said. "The three elements necessary to become a suspect. Means and opportunity are there already. Now we've got motive."

Hogan was perfectly right, of course. Bunny had admitted she'd been on the TenHuis premises when Abigail began to bang on the door. Although it was after closing hours, Abigail had seen the lights inside, and she wanted in.

Bunny claimed that she had hidden in the back, even going through the door that accessed the Clown Building, to get away from Abigail. She had waited until Abigail left, then snuck outside.

What if, instead, she had admitted Abigail? That late on a winter evening it was unlikely that anyone would have seen her let Abigail in.

Abigail could have told Bunny that her will had been made. Bunny would then have known she was officially Abigail's heir. That was motive.

Letting Abigail into the TenHuis shop would have given Bunny opportunity. And Bunny had had Dolly's keys. One of them would open the padlock that kept the door between the stores shut.

If Bunny then killed Abigail—well, that didn't sound like the Bunny I knew, but did I really know anything about Bunny? Though I felt deep sympathy for her, as Joe did, we had known her only a few months.

And certainly Bunny would have access to the means used to kill Abigail. The detectives hadn't

identified the weapon used in her death, but there were
dozens of items on any construction site that could
have been used to hand out a fatal head injury.

Hogan instructed me to say nothing about the will;
he said he was going to call Joe himself, after he talked
to the state police.

I walked back to the TenHuis shop. I was extremely
disheartened. My Texas grandmother would have said
my tail feathers were dragging.

I'd been worried about Bunny being left penniless
because Beau was such a jerk. Now that fear seemed
to be lightened. But a far greater danger had replaced
my concern. She could be left in prison.

It was a mess. What could I do about it?

Hogan would say I could do nothing. But maybe I
could do something. What?

As I neared the shop, I saw a curtain twitch in Dolly's apartment. So she was home. I wondered where
she had been.

Several people seemed to have been out of town
over Friday night, plus for the weekend.

Where had Beau and Anya gone? They had apparently known nothing about Abigail's death. Beau had
been back shortly after eight o'clock that morning,
when I saw him at the post office. He might even have
returned late the previous evening. But where had he
and Anya been?

I stopped in front of the wine shop. Anya worked
there. It didn't look crowded.

I could, I told myself, stop in to buy a bottle of Michigan red. I was sure Anya would be there. Maybe I
could ask her where Beau had been the night before.

I made a hard right and went into the store. Anya
gave me a wave from behind the counter. She was

putting two bottles of Fenn Valley Capriccio into one of the fancy carriers the shop used, waiting on a couple whose snazzy ski jackets indicated they were tourists. I looked through a bin of wine, waiting for her to be free.

The Warner River Wine Shop was touristy to the max. It had a mural of a vineyard on the back wall. There were displays of wineglasses, carafes, cork pullers, coasters, and other wine paraphernalia on tables down the center. On the right and left the walls were covered with shelving arranged in diamond-shaped bins and stocked with local wines. A wine-colored curtain hung over a door behind the cash register. Vines adorned with plastic grapes and their leaves were looped around the ceiling.

The store had a fresh, bright atmosphere. It pictured vineyards as perfect places for family picnics.

It almost seemed that the only thing out of place was the ultralush Anya Hartley. Her lipstick too bright, her hair too dark, her figure too full, her clothes too gaudy and too tight. To me she always looked like a stripper in street clothes. It wasn't a wholesome look.

How did I ask her where she'd been over the weekend? It might turn out to be a weekend pole-dancing retreat. It might also turn out to be a church camp, I reminded myself. You never can tell by looking at people.

Anya and I greeted each other. "What can I get for you?" she asked. "You're a white wine fan, right?"

"I'm trying to widen my horizons. What kind of pinot noir do you recommend?"

We discussed the various pinot noirs. The Warner River Wine Shop was too small to hold a large stock, of course, but there was some variety, and Anya immediately offered to order more.

I settled for two bottles, one each of two different brands.

As I handed Anya my credit card, I tried a little chitchat. "Where was everybody this weekend? The whole town seemed deserted."

"Oh, I guess we all try to get out of town."

"Sure. But what did you find to do? Everything seems pretty dull around here in the winter."

"Beau and I went over to Augusta. We turned off our phones. We didn't even hear about his bitchy aunt until we got back."

"That must have been a shocker."

"Yes. Beau was knocked flat. Some people say that 'only the good die young.' But that woman should have been dead years ago."

Was Anya nuts? How could she talk that way about a murder victim? Didn't she know it was rude? Also dumb? Either was likely to make her a suspect in a murder.

I tried to make a noncommittal response. "Well, I've heard that Abigail Birdsong was a big help to Beau as an artist."

"Huh! She was a pain in the butt to him as an artist! She kept him on a tight leash. She picked what art shows he could enter. She bought him stuff, true. Like a van, for example. But it wasn't necessarily what he would have bought himself. She was a real tightwad. And it was a struggle to keep her from picking out his clothes and deciding the menu if he and Bunny gave a dinner party."

"She picked out Beau's clothes? That does seem extreme, but I guess she meant well."

Anya gave a harsh laugh. "She meant to keep Beau

as a puppet. She claimed she could advise him on his art!"

"I guess his artwork sells pretty well."

"Not as well as it would if he'd given his imagination free rein! Have you seen the Orchid series?"

She handed me my wine, nearly knocking my carrier over, and yanked a cell phone from under the counter. "Look at these! They're really stunning! Just thumb through them."

I thumbed. Stunning, I agreed, was a good description. That and ugly. The work made my eyes cross, and not with pleasure.

Each of the paintings was a portrait of a nude model. Looking closely, I decided each was Anya. And each, to my way of thinking, was absolutely hideous. The colors were harsh and ugly. The model's body was misshapen. Yet the paintings were apparently intended to be representational. They made me think of cartoons. But they weren't cartoons.

The work was so different from the large flowers Beau had painted earlier that it was hard to visualize what effect he must have been trying for.

I tried to be polite. "They're certainly interesting," I said.

"But that idiot Abigail Birdsong didn't like them!" Anya said. "She was pushing Beau to paint the trash he'd always painted."

I smiled, took the handle of my wine carrier. "I guess his earlier style was quite successful."

"It was smothering Beau's artistic sensibilities," Anya said. "He was choking. Now he can . . ."

"Anya!"

The call for Anya came so unexpectedly that I

jumped and both my bottles of wine fell on their side in the center of the sales counter. Luckily neither broke.

Andrew Hartley's head popped out from the door behind Anya.

"Anya," he said. Now his voice was soft. He looked pained. "Would you please go to the bank while things are slow?"

Anya gave him a glare that could burn a zigzag down his face. But she put on a bright red ski jacket and a boldly checked black and white scarf. Before I could react, she grabbed a cash bag from under the counter and was out the door.

I picked up my wine carrier. "Hello, Andrew. I didn't mean to distract Anya from her duties."

"She's pretty easily distracted, Lee." He still looked pained. "Could I ask you a favor?"

"Of course."

"I know you're related to the police chief."

I smiled. "Don't ask me to give him advice. I assure you it would be useless. Hogan thinks for himself."

"I know that. But I'd appreciate your not mentioning Anya's latest tirade to him."

"Oh, he collects his own testimony. He won't ask me about it."

"Anya—well, she's more upset over Miss Birdsong's death than she admits. I'd rather she had an opportunity to calm down before—well, in case Chief Jones wants her to make a statement."

He came out into the shop and leaned on the counter, shaking his head. "I guess I'll always be the big brother, and Anya will always be the naughty little sister."

I felt sorry for him. If Anya acted like this to strangers, she must be hell on wheels in the home circle.

"Don't worry, Andrew," I said. "My lips are sealed."

Chapter 11

I was confused as I walked to TenHuis Chocolade. Had I promised not to say anything about Anya's tirade? I hadn't intended to do that. I don't keep things from Hogan or from Joe. I trust both of them not to misuse information.

On the other hand, just as a person, I try not to repeat things that make other people look bad. It's a habit too close to gossip. And us small-town girls understand how destructive gossip is.

What had possessed Anya anyway? She must be crazy to go into a fit like that, berating Abigail. Even if she didn't obey the convention of not speaking ill of the dead, it was simply stupid to make herself look small-minded and—well, tacky.

Though Anya did look tacky a lot of the time, I thought tackily. Meow, meow.

I had my hand on the door of TenHuis before I realized I was hungry. I went inside and walked back to

Bunny's office. Things were quiet, she said. She had plenty of e-mail orders to work on, and she was saving them for me to check before she sent them back to the workshop to be filled. So I told her I was going to the Sidewalk to pick up a sandwich to eat at my desk, and I left again.

By that time it was after one o'clock, and the lunch crowd was gone. At the Sidewalk I asked for a turkey sandwich to go, then sat at a table near the front door. In that spot I could talk to Lindy Herrera while I waited.

"Some excitement you've had at TenHuis," Lindy said. "Is it all settling down?"

"I have no idea. I know Hogan still has the Clown Building closed off." I went on reluctantly. "Plus part of our building. The whole thing's nonsensical, as far as I can see."

Lindy and I had already chewed this topic over. I didn't want to talk about it anymore. So I changed the subject. "How's Tony Junior doing? I mean TJ! I keep forgetting he wants to use his new nickname."

Lindy's three kids were always good for a report. I looked at her and nodded while she told me what they were up to. Lindy and I were the same age, but she married at seventeen and her children were already in their teens. I'd been married twice, and I was into my thirties, but I had no kids.

I pretended to listen to Lindy, but she could have been talking about anything. I wasn't hearing what she said. My brain was racing with questions about Abigail's death.

Why had the killer apparently taken Abigail into the rarely used stairwell to attack her? Would Abigail have gone there willingly? Why had her attacker laid her body out neatly in the Clown Building? What had he—or she—used as a weapon in killing her? I went around and around, asking myself these questions over and over.

Then Lindy's voice caught my attention. "But I don't know if he followed her, or it was merely a coincidence," she said. "Do you think I should tell Hogan?"

Huh?

"Let's go back a minute," I said. "Please start over when you stopped talking about your kids."

Lindy frowned. "Lee, that was five minutes ago."

"I'm sorry. My mind was buzzing around the ceiling. Did you say someone followed Abigail Birdsong out of here Friday night?"

"Not exactly." Lindy sighed deeply. "I said she was in here Friday night. Alone. And she griped about the music. The way she always does. I mean, did. She always wanted it turned down."

"Her usual act?"

"Yep. She ordered beef stew. Then she had coffee after dinner, which was unusual for her. She usually gulps her food and rushes out the door."

"Was she waiting for someone?"

"I don't think so. She wrote something while she was waiting for her food, and she worked on it some more over coffee."

"Oh." No surprise there.

"Miss Birdsong had a big plastic sack from the drugstore with her. She pulled stuff out of it—a yellow tablet and a new pen. I know it was a new one, because she scribbled all over the pad. I guess she was making sure the pen was writing okay. She ripped that page off and wrote a page or two on the tablet. Then she got

Felix and Liz to sign whatever it was. I suppose as witnesses."

All of this was not surprising. Hogan and I had guessed as much from the holographic will.

"By then," Lindy said, "I was working on balancing. You know, at my desk in the alcove off the kitchen. Miss Birdsong asked Liz if there was such a thing as a Post-it in the place. Liz came back and got one from me and took it to her."

Again, that checked out. She'd written her note to me on a yellow Post-it. Nothing exciting there.

"The next time Liz came through to the kitchen," Lindy said, "she told me Miss Birdsong apparently had some important piece of mail. Now she wanted a stamp."

"Did you give her one?"

"Yes." Lindy laughed. "I didn't even add it to her bill. I offered to take her mail to the post office. I was dropping off some of my own mail anyway, and the stamp had come from my own supply. The business mail goes through Mike's office, not down here."

"Did Abigail take you up on that?"

"She did. I was surprised. She had acted as if this paper she was writing was such a big deal that I had expected that she'd insist on mailing the result herself."

Lindy frowned a minute. "You know, looking back, maybe she really was planning to meet someone."

"Why do you say that?"

"Because she drank coffee until nine o'clock exactly. That's when we close, so I was keeping an eye on the time. In fact, I went up front and locked the door then. I didn't ask her to leave, but I'd barely turned the lock when Miss Birdsong got up from her table, put on her jacket, pulled her cap on, and went to the front door. Maybe that was because it was exactly nine o'clock."

"You mean she had arranged to meet somebody at nine. But it could mean she simply had realized that it was closing time."

"There were several tables still occupied. We were cleaning up, but we didn't rush anybody. When she got ready to go, I saw she was holding the letter. So I asked if she wanted me to add it to my mail. I had just put her letter in the stack with mine when I saw her meeting someone outside."

"Oh, Lindy! Have you told Hogan this?"

"Not yet."

"You call him and tell him about this. Right away."

"But I didn't see who it was."

"What did he look like?"

"Like a person wearing a winter jacket with a hood in the dark! I didn't get a good look at him. Or her."

"Maybe not, but for starters, did you think it was a man?"

"Lee, this is February in Michigan! It was a figure in a parka. It could have been a man, a woman, or a teenager. All I know is that it wasn't a small child. And he didn't have a limp or a wheelchair or anything distinctive. All I saw was two figures in big jackets—Miss Birdsong and this other person."

"Did you see them walk away?"

"Yes, and they went down toward your place. But I didn't watch them go. They could have turned at the corner."

My sandwich came then, and I paid for it and left. But as I went out I asked one more question. "That sheet of paper Miss Birdsong wrote on to test her pen— did it get thrown out?"

"Sure."

"Too bad. She might have written something important on it."

"A clue? I don't think so. It was just scribbling."

Lindy promised that she would call Hogan immediately, and I left. Her story might be a real lead. Maybe the Warner Pier patrolman had even seen someone on the street or had noted a car he recognized parked in this block.

Though that might not mean much. After all, Lindy had said there were still several tables in use at the Sidewalk Café when Abigail left. Those people would be parking downtown. Plus the restaurant's help would be parking on the street this time of the year.

I tried to calm myself. The whole episode might mean nothing, and I needed to do some work at my real job.

This time I made it back to my office, where I found Bunny in a complete tizzy.

She ran up to my office as soon as I walked in. "Oh, Lee! Hogan came by. He says you found a will Abigail had made."

"Yes, I did, Bunny. I thought it was evidence, so I took it to him. He asked me not to say anything about it until he had checked it out."

"I guess he did that, because he says he talked to Joe and to Abigail's lawyer. And he says she left everything to me! To me!"

"I know, Bunny. I was awfully surprised that she made a holographic will. But she had told you she was going to leave her estate to you."

"But I didn't think she'd do it. Beau was everything to her."

"Bunny, don't get too excited. Frankly, this is the

sort of will that leads to lawsuits. So don't spend the money yet."

"I don't want to spend it at all! I'm terribly sorry she did that. I'll just give it to Beau."

"Oh, Bunny! Don't do that without talking to Joe! There are all sorts of legal ramifications to something like this. Please listen to his advice."

I didn't go into details, but the most obvious ramification was that Bunny might not get the money for a long time if she was accused of killing Abigail. That would also take a long, long time to sort out, even if she weren't ultimately convicted.

Bunny went back to her office, stumbling on the step as she walked. I felt glad that she didn't have to handle chocolate kettles and vats that afternoon. She was a nervous wreck.

So I wasn't surprised when I heard a crash. This was no minor bump. This was a real ring-a-ding rattle-clang bing-bonger. Something big and metal had been knocked over or dropped.

That was Bunny's signature sound. I groaned. It sounded like something expensive this time.

I went out into the shop and gawked through the doorway into the workroom. All the hairnet ladies were looking toward the Clown Building.

And there I saw the mess. A large kettle was lying on its side near the padlocked door. The kettle was rolling gently back and forth, gushing dark chocolate with each roll.

But the person standing over it, horror in every gesture, was not Bunny. It was Dolly Jolly.

"Oh my goodness!" Dolly boomed. "I've done it this time!"

I resisted the impulse to get involved. Not only did

I not want to, but also the workroom was Aunt Nettie's domain. I could already hear her speaking briskly. "We need a dishpan over here. And several sponges. Pails and mops."

"I'm so sorry, Nettie!"

"It's all right, Dolly. You've handled gallons and gallons of chocolate without dripping a drop. The world won't come to an end because of a spill."

"An awful big spill!"

"We'll survive. Nadine! Make us a big bucket of soapy water."

I turned toward my office, then saw that Bunny was coming toward me. She had been nowhere near the big spill. When she was close to me, she whispered, "Thank goodness I didn't do that."

"I didn't do it either," I said.

I heard nothing more about the death of Abigail Birdsong until five o'clock, though I certainly thought about it. Instead I tried to work. As I went over the e-mail orders with Bunny and performed other chores, she told me she was calmer tonight, and she didn't think she'd spend the night with Joe and me.

"I'll leave your sheets on the bed," I said. "You might change your mind."

The afternoon went by. The final person I spoke to before leaving was Dolly. I called her over and made her sit in my visitor's chair.

"Dolly, have the detectives moved you out of your apartment?"

She lowered her usual shout a few decibels when she answered. "They suggested that, but I want to stay there!"

"How about coming out to stay with us?"

Again she shook her head. "No, I like being in my

own home! I don't want to leave! They promised that they'd make frequent patrols of this block!"

"Well, I'm going to invite Chayslee again, too. I'm real nervous about these two buildings."

"I feel bad about spilling all that chocolate!" she said. "You ought to dock my pay!"

"Aw, come on, Dolly! Do you know how much chocolate your efficiency has saved us in the years you've worked here? We still owe you big-time."

"But I still owe you for the labor of mopping it up!"

"Did Aunt Nettie say anything about that?"

"No. She's too nice!" Dolly shook her head. "Oh gosh, Lee. This has simply been an awful day!"

"I'm sorry, Dolly. Is it your mom?"

"No, no. Mom's fine! You know, not well, but coping! I went to see her Friday! Then Saturday I just went to Grand Rapids and prowled the malls, trying to get my mind off my troubles! I'm upset about a friend!"

"I'm here if you want to talk. But be careful about friends. I don't want you to tell me any secrets."

"No secrets would be involved! It's just that the two of us had become quite close, and now we seem to be on different wavelengths all of a sudden!" Dolly stared at the floor. She sighed deeply. "Well, I guess I need to talk to my pal before I . . ." Her voice trailed off, and she looked up and smiled broadly.

"Before I squeal!" she said. "Oink! Oink!" She made pig noises and wrinkled her nose up. We both giggled.

Chapter 12

I didn't give Dolly's concerns a lot of thought. Frankly, if I worried about anybody, it was Bunny. We'd heard nothing more from Hogan, but as far as I could see Bunny was still in danger of arrest.

Again I asked Chayslee to stay at our house that night. She declined. Like Dolly, she said she was staying in her apartment. But in her case a friend was spending the night with her. "We'll set a trap of some sort," she said. "Maybe pots and pans that will fall. And we'll call the cops before we answer the door, no matter who's outside."

Bunny stuck to her plan to stay in the room she rented, so we didn't hear anything more from her either.

It started as an uneventful evening. Joe and I went out for dinner, and I realized that I had memorized the entire menu of the Sidewalk Café. Somehow that made the food seem less appealing. Lindy came over to our table to tell us she'd talked to Hogan, telling him about Abigail Birdsong meeting someone outside the restaurant and about her writing the will as she drank after-dinner coffee. Hogan hadn't commented. We didn't either. The dinner hour was not exciting.

But as the meal went on, I mentioned to Joe that no one—not Dolly, not Bunny, not Chayslee—was interested in either of our guest rooms. I detailed their excuses.

"Personally, I'm just as happy not having a slumber party," Joe said. "But Dolly's excuses are a little worrying."

"That she's quarreled with a friend? Why does that worry you?"

"Dolly never struck me as having a whole lot of social life, so I hate to see her quarrel with any of her friends. But despite her being such a homebody, everybody seems to like her. It's kind of odd, having few friends and also being well liked."

"I think you're mistaken, Joe. Dolly has lots of friends. I don't think she ever lacks for someone to go out to dinner or see a movie with."

"I'm sure that's right. I guess I'm being a male chauvinist. I just don't see Dolly as—well, part of a couple. If a guy from the office wanted me to fix him up with a date, I wouldn't suggest Dolly."

I dropped my eyes to my vegetable plate, and I pictured Dolly: more than six feet tall, probably weighing more than two hundred pounds, crazy red hair, and— yes, let's admit it—plain of face.

But she was a wonderful person. I felt sad. Did Dolly miss having a man in her life? Was Dolly lonely? She didn't deserve to be.

Then I looked up at Joe. He was giving a rueful smile.

"Men are shallow," he said.

His remark exactly echoed what I'd been thinking. We both smiled. "So are women," I said.

I felt a pang of guilt, but I felt happy that I had Joe. As far as looks go, I admitted to myself that I first noticed him because of those fabulous shoulders and secondly because of his handsome puss.

Yes, I had been shallow, too. But I was only sixteen the first time I met Joe. He'd been lifeguard at Warner Pier Beach in those days, and I'd been a summer counter girl for my aunt and uncle's shop. On my days off I hung around the lifeguard's station, feeling skinny and unattractive. Joe never seemed to notice me, and I certainly didn't waste time pining over him. It was more than ten years later when things sparked between us. And the sparks led me to discover he had other qualities, such as kindness and intelligence. Stuff that is a lot more important than shoulders or good looks.

This exchange gave me a nice reminiscence that included gratitude to my mother. She'd been the one who insisted that I join the "charm school" class that had ended several years later with me in a Miss Texas competition. Even an awkward, almost six-foot-tall blonde with invisible eyelashes can learn to look good and can develop confidence with the right kind of encouragement.

But it made me worry about Dolly again. I decided I should talk to her. Extend the conversation we'd had earlier.

Joe and I had two cars that night, so when we left the restaurant I told him that if he'd go on, I'd drop by Dolly's place before I drove myself home.

"Don't be too long," he said. And he waggled his eyebrows and gave me a kiss. Yes, I'm glad I've got him.

The Sidewalk Café is just half a block from TenHuis Chocolade, and Dolly lives over TenHuis. So I walked to her apartment.

It was another cold, crisp night. I was dressed in full woolies: long johns, lined boots, blue jeans, flannel shirt, ski jacket, knitted cap. Since I was heavily laden with clothes, walking was sort of fun. I hummed a bit as I rounded the corner and headed toward Dolly's front door.

And ahead, on the sidewalk outside her apartment, I saw a kneeling figure.

I was so startled that I stopped dead, staring, instead of running forward as I should have. Surely my eyes were deceiving me. There couldn't be anything wrong.

Then something moved. An angular something like an arm went up. Another arm flopped out onto the sidewalk.

And I realized the first arm ended in a hand, and the hand was holding a stick of some sort.

The huddled shape was made up of two people. One was lying on the sidewalk, and the other was about to hit him.

I screamed at the top of my lungs.

Instantly one of the figures on the sidewalk jumped to its feet. I screamed again. The figure turned and began running toward me.

Then I let out a real shriek, the kind that wakes the dead. I whirled and began running back the way I'd come.

I suppose I was going as fast as I could. Or at least as fast as I could go on an icy sidewalk. Which was only one problem with any kind of a chase scene in downtown Warner Pier on a February evening.

It was not only slippery, it was also dark, and it was lonely.

The stores were closed. The streetlights were dim. And in a summer resort like Warner Pier—in wintertime—I could yell for help like a train whistle, and the likelihood of being heard was fifty-fifty. There just might not be anybody around to listen.

I could feel the person chasing me, and he was closing in.

I kept running, slipping, and sliding, and finally—right across the street from the Downtown Drug Store—I hit a patch of ice that did me in. I went flying across the sidewalk like an Olympic figure skater in slow motion. I hit a light pole, grabbed it with one hand, and swung around. Then I slowly sank to the sidewalk, landing on my keister. That's when the miracle happened.

I finally remembered my key chain. I pulled it from the side pocket of my purse and hit the little alarm that's attached to it.

Woo-ah, woo-ah, woo-ah!

The person chasing me did a pirouette and took off in the opposite direction.

I lifted myself to my feet, with both me and the alarm still shrieking. Then I walked—not ran—back toward Dolly's apartment. When I reached the figure lying on the sidewalk, I dropped to my knees and looked at the victim. There was enough light to see the color of the person's hair.

Bright red. It was Dolly.

She was breathing, but her breathing was shallow.

What followed was a jumble. I called 9-1-1. I called

Joe. I pulled off my jacket and tried to use it to shield Dolly's head from the ice-cold sidewalk. Joe came back. Two patrol cars came. The local ambulance came. They gave my jacket back. Chayslee looked out her window, then she and her friend Mary came down the stairs. Andrew Hartley came down from his apartment. Hogan and Aunt Nettie showed up. There was a huge commotion.

I told Hogan I didn't see the attacker well enough to know if it was a man, a woman, or an older teenager. The weapon he/she held might have been a pipe or a stick or a board.

"All I can remember is some big black and white checks," I said. "It could have been the trim on a jacket. I don't think it was a cap."

I was no help at all.

Dolly was stirring a little by the time the local ambulance crew got there. Within five minutes, they had her on the way to the hospital in Holland. Pretty good for a volunteer team.

Aunt Nettie and I were standing on the sidewalk in front of TenHuis, clinging to each other, with Joe hugging both of us.

And Hogan came over. "Lee, Nettie, maybe you two had better look your shop over. Can you ladies do that?"

I realized I was crying. I sniffed, blew my nose, and tried to buck up.

"Sure we can do it," I said.

"Yes, Hogan," Aunt Nettie said. "We'll check things right now."

"Good. Then could you check Dolly's apartment? I've sent a detective up there, but maybe you two could see if there's anything odd, out of place."

I tried to sound calm. "Of course, Hogan."

Aunt Nettie brought out her keys and unlocked the front door to the shop. She, Joe, and I went in.

"What on earth could have happened?" she asked.

Neither Joe nor I answered, and she spoke again. "This place looks normal."

"I don't understand any of this!" I said.

Aunt Nettie's first observation seemed to be correct. The shop looked to be untouched. Everything was locked, including the door into the Clown Building, my desk, and other things that would normally be closed up. The break room looked no messier than usual. Despite the mopping that went on at closing time every day, there were muddy footprints near the back door. As usual the three of us used the street door to Dolly's apartment to troop upstairs for a check there. The detective who met us said the front door to the apartment had been standing open, as if Dolly had fled outside. He warned us that we shouldn't touch anything if we could avoid it.

As we reached the top of the steep stairs, I realized it had been at least a year since I had been up them. That seemed awful, somehow. Dolly relaxed, cooked, watched television, and slept right over my head.

I considered her a friend. Yet I rarely saw her except at work. We didn't even go to lunch often.

When I expressed my feelings to Joe, he smiled. "Maybe eight hours a day is enough," he said. "There's no reason to live in the pocket of someone you work with."

Dolly's apartment was as neat as the gorgeous truffles and bonbons she made. She is efficient to the core, and TenHuis takes full advantage of that trait.

The apartment was very ordinary. If you come up

the front stairs, you pass through a glass door. This enters onto a small foyer, located in the center of the building. The foyer opens into the living-dining room.

The apartment has one unusual feature. As Dolly had pointed out earlier, the living room is at the back, overlooking the alley, and the bedroom in the front.

The living room is separated from the kitchen only by what HGTV calls a "peninsula," an island attached to the wall or to a counter at one end. Dolly's had stools and could be used for a breakfast bar.

Actually I thought that Dolly used it for extra cooking space. Her canisters were stored at one end of it, for example, and so was a large electric mixer.

If you turned right from the foyer, a short hallway led to the bathroom and bedroom. The door to the back stairway, the one where Abigail had apparently been killed, opened off that foyer, too. Except that it rarely opened. That door was always locked, as nearly as I could tell.

Nothing was obviously out of place in Dolly's apartment; every sofa cushion, throw rug, crystal vase, and book seemed to nestle into its proper spot. The bathroom had fresh hand towels, the rows of flowers printed on the bedspread marched exactly down the edge of the bed, and the closet door was closed. The only unusual thing I noticed was a copy of *Sports Illustrated*. I'd never heard Dolly talk about sports, but it was neatly lined up on the coffee table.

I almost cried when I saw the place. Dolly was such a big woman—tall and hefty and with a loud voice. Yet her apartment looked as if the daintiest woman in the world lived there. There were flowers on the couch upholstery, the color scheme was all in pastels, and her dishes were a beautiful shade of rose.

Hand-painted china cups were displayed on a whatnot shelf. She had a nice display of crystal pieces.

It was as if a little girl ballerina lived there. Maybe one did—the ultrafeminine little girl inside the big girl who was Dolly.

"I don't see anything out of order," I said. Joe nodded in agreement, but Aunt Nettie spoke. "Do you smell something?"

Joe and I answered in unison. "Coffee!"

We all three turned to the kitchen. It was as neat and clean as the rest of the place. But an expensive electric Chemex coffeemaker sat on the counter. Its carafe was almost full of coffee.

"Sure smells better than what we have in the break room," I said.

"It's an eight-cup pot," Aunt Nettie said. She opened the cupboard. "No coffee here."

"You know Dolly and her saving ways," I said. "She probably didn't make a big pot of coffee every day. Maybe she kept her coffee in the freezer."

Sure enough, we found both decaf and regular coffee beans in the freezer compartment of Dolly's refrigerator. In a cupboard we found a coffee grinder.

"Wow!" Joe said. "You should have her in charge of the break room."

"She's too valuable making chocolate," Aunt Nettie said.

"Clean hand towels and a big pot of coffee," I said. "So we know she was expecting a guest."

Joe and Aunt Nettie nodded in agreement. "I'd say he or she had arrived," Joe said. "The lab techs will check for any evidence, but it looks as if she let her attacker in."

"Who could it have been?" Aunt Nettie asked. She unplugged the Chemex pot.

"Could it have been a male friend?" I asked. I walked to the coffee table and picked up the *Sports Illustrated*. "Or am I being sexist?" Neither Joe nor Aunt Nettie replied.

Who could have been coming by Dolly's apartment? Tears welled in my eyes. How could I have worked with Dolly every day, how could I have regarded her so highly, and not known who her friends were? The three of us seemed to sink into sadness.

The detective cleared his throat, and it roused us.

"Come on," Joe said. "Let's head for the hospital."

I made one stop before we left, checking TenHuis records for the name and address of Dolly's next of kin. Instead of her mom, it was a sister in Clinton, Michigan.

When I read the name, I spoke. "You've got to be kidding."

"What?" Aunt Nettie asked.

"Dolly's sister's name is Molly," I said. "She must be married. Her last name is Jefferson. But until she took her vows, it was the Jolly sisters, Molly and Dolly."

"No doubt there's a brother named Wally and an auntie named Polly," Joe said. "Let's head for Holland."

The three of us climbed into Joe's truck, and he aimed it toward Holland and the hospital's emergency room.

Hogan and a state police detective were in the waiting area. They said they knew nothing about Dolly yet. She had still been unconscious when she arrived at the hospital.

Hogan said the police had found a short piece of pipe lying in the gutter. This seemed likely as a weapon. But it was the type of item found in a Dumpster. Dolly's attacker could have picked it up anyplace. Not much of a clue as to where it came from.

I settled down for a wait, telling Aunt Nettie she should go home.

"You, too, Joe," I said. "I'll stay tonight. Should I call Dolly's sister?"

"I'll handle that," Hogan said. "Make it official." I gave him the number.

Nobody else moved. I'd given my orders, and they got the usual reaction. Everybody ignored them. So we all sat there. Nobody had much to say. We were all sitting an hour later when I felt the cold blast of air that means someone has entered the emergency room's waiting area. When I looked up I saw Lindy.

"Hey!" I said. "What are you doing here?"

"You're not the only ones worried about Dolly," she said. "How's she doing?"

Hogan had the latest report, so we all looked at him. "Still unconscious," he said. "No worse. What have you got there?"

I noticed then that Lindy was holding a paper sack. She shook it triumphantly.

"Yahoo!" she said. "I spent two hours going through the Dumpster at the Sidewalk Café, and I think I found the sheet of paper that Abigail Birdsong threw out after she wrote her will."

Who's Who in Chocolate

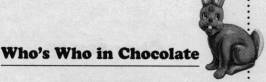

SAMUEL PEPYS

Pepys is known as a great diarist of the 1600s. He didn't invent, import, or prepare chocolate. But he drank a lot of it, and he described a new social institution in England—the coffee house, which also offered chocolate. Plus political gossip.

Chocolate, of course, was strictly a drink at this time. It was already popular elsewhere in Europe. But the English coffee houses were designed to appeal not to the upper classes, but to anyone who could afford a cup.

Pepys was born into the middle class, but worked his way up to become secretary of the Admiralty. He was also president of the Royal Society, the country's leading scientific organization, and was a friend and confidant to Charles II.

In his famed diary, he repeatedly tells of drinking chocolate—sometimes he called it "jocolatte."

The coffee houses developed into the gentlemen's clubs of the day and contributed to the formation of political parties, since like-minded men gathered at the same coffee houses.

Chapter 13

Lindy handed the sack to Hogan. "And I can't see that anything on the page makes a bit of sense."

Her remarks were something of a letdown, of course. Ever since I'd heard that Abigail had written something at the same time she wrote her will, I'd hoped that it would be something important. "Joe Doakes is my murderer," maybe. Or "the holographic will was written under duress."

But apparently that was not the case. And apparently we were not to learn anything about it anyway. Hogan merely nodded and said, "Thanks, Lindy. Finding something that has any meaning was always a long shot. I'll get the lab to go over it. Even if there's nothing significant written on the page, it may contain a fingerprint or other evidence that could mean something."

"I can guarantee that it doesn't," Lindy said.

"Contain a fingerprint, I mean. No one except the waiter approached her the whole time she worked on it."

"Anyway, we've got it," Hogan said. "And you were a real trouper to look through that Dumpster." He stood up. "I'll try to get a new report."

As soon as he walked away, I grabbed Lindy and spoke in a low voice. "Okay, what did it say?"

"Nothing I could give any meaning to, Lee."

"I understand. But what was it?"

"Well, there were a bunch of those things my grandma called 'push-pulls' and 'ovals.' It's some sort of a penmanship exercise. They were dropped from the curriculum by the time we were in grade school."

"I know what you mean. Little doodads in rows. Abigail must have made those when she was testing her new pen. Did she write any words?"

"It was all just gibberish, Lee. There was an occasional word written as if she was testing the spelling. She had written the word 'Culpepper' with two spellings, for example. Is the name Culpepper in the will?"

I nodded. "That was Bunny's maiden name. Anything else?"

"There was a sort of list. Each item had a dash in front of it. But the actual items—well, they didn't make sense."

"None?"

"Unless you can decipher code. They seemed to be initials or symbols. One looked like an ampersand."

"What were the initials?"

"There was an *A*, a capital *A*. That was followed by the word 'beneficiary.' The next line had another dash, followed by a capital *B*. That had a note reading 'out.' There was only one full name, and I didn't recognize that."

"What was the name?"

"It was crazy. Ambruster Hayworth."

"Who on earth is that?"

Joe spoke then. "You gals had better stop speculating. Here comes Hogan, and I'm sure he'd rather work on this himself."

"Lindy," I said aloud, "they've got some coffee over there. Do you want to try a cup?"

That's the way the rest of the night went. We all urged one another to go home. None of Dolly's friends budged, though most of the detectives left. We drank a lot of coffee, told a few Dolly stories, laughed at some of them, and cried at others.

I told about the hobo jungle where I first met Dolly. Dolly didn't live in the hobo jungle, but the path that led from the interstate to the jungle ran along the edge of her yard. Dolly used to put sack lunches out there for her wandering neighbors.

"She always included homemade cookies," I said. "Dolly was never afraid of the men. And she figured that if they were there, they needed food. Dolly simply can't stand to see anybody hungry."

It was a long night.

It was nearly eight a.m.—still dark—when Andrew Hartley and Chayslee Zimmerman showed up the next morning.

"Hey!" I said. "Is our block still barricaded?"

"Just a cop car in the street and one in the alley," Chayslee said. "I nearly came here last night, but I hated to leave Mary there alone, and she had to be at work at six thirty. How's Dolly doing?"

"She'll be shipped to a Grand Rapids hospital pretty

soon," Hogan said. "They want her to see a specialist there."

That was news to me, but I didn't question Hogan.

Instead I turned to Andrew. "Andrew, I didn't even know that you'd ever met Dolly."

"We're neighbors!" he said. "I'm living in the apartment over Warner River Wine."

I knew that, of course. And I'd seen him the night before, when he joined the crowd checking on what had caused the commotion I'd made with my key chain alarm.

"Now I remember. You came down last night to check on her. It was darn cold there, and you didn't look as if you were dressed warmly enough."

Andrew gave me a sharp look. "I ran out in a hurry," he said. "I'm really concerned about Dolly. She's great, of course. I'd barely moved in when Dolly dropped over to say hi. With homemade cookies and TenHuis chocolates, of course. Plus, she's a genius about wine. All kinds of food lore. She's helped me immeasurably."

He turned his back on me and sat next to Hogan, asking questions. How was Dolly doing? Had the police gotten a statement from her? When did they expect her to be able to give a statement? Did they have any hint of who might have attacked her? His voice was pleasant; I nearly dozed off.

Hogan's answers were noncommittal, but he said Dolly was still unconscious. After a few minutes Andrew seemed to give up on getting information.

"I'll sure put her at the top of my own prayer list and the one at my church," he said. "Is there anything I can do for her right now?"

"Not that I know of," Hogan said. "Lee's keeping a list of people who call or come by."

"Make sure my name's on it," Andrew said. "I wouldn't want Dolly to think I didn't care about her. Not after all she's done to help me."

Chayslee sat with Lindy and me, joining in the praise for Dolly, citing her friendliness as she was getting settled in Warner Pier. She also asked to be kept in the loop with news of Dolly.

Andrew and Chayslee left soon after that, both saying they had to go to work in an hour or so.

I didn't have a chance to ask Andrew which church he attended. Small-town America—in Texas or "up North"—is loaded with little churches, and big ones.

Andrew and Chayslee had barely gone when more people showed up—Barbara from the bank; Greg Glossop, druggist and Warner Pier's most active gossip; and several others from the downtown business community. I was surprised that Mike Westerly was among them. The construction worker had seemed very rattled after he discovered Abigail Birdsong's body. I wouldn't have expected him to deliberately seek out people linked to a similar crime. But there he was, asking how Dolly was doing.

None of them stayed long, but they had each driven thirty miles to get there.

Joe nudged me. "What was it we were saying earlier? About Dolly not having many friends?"

"I guess I was saying I wasn't a very good friend to her."

He put his arm around my shoulders.

Aunt Nettie had taken an hour's nap by then, but she still seemed exhausted. The rest of us ran out of conversation. Then the quiet was broken by a piercing voice.

"Where's Dolly? Where is she? Dolly Jolly?"

Hogan sighed deeply and stood up. "Here we go," he said. He gestured to Aunt Nettie, and she stood up, too.

They walked across the room, and I watched their progress, trying to understand just what was going on.

At the desk I saw a tall red-haired woman. She was nearly six feet tall and had red hair, but this woman was nothing like Dolly. Still, she was squawking for Dolly to be produced. Could she be Dolly's sister, Molly?

Hogan approached the woman and spoke quietly to her. I assumed that he introduced Aunt Nettie and himself, but his voice was so low that I couldn't swear to that. Then he led the newcomer straight through the doors to the treatment area, with Aunt Nettie trailing along.

"I guess that's Dolly's sister," I said. "They don't look much alike. Despite the hair."

"There's only one Dolly," Lindy said. "But that woman does look familiar. Has she ever been to Warner Pier?"

"I don't remember hearing of a visit from her," I said, "and I'm sure I've never met her."

Lindy shook her head. "I don't remember any of Dolly's family coming to see her. I've always thought it was sort of odd."

"I know what you mean. Dolly goes to see them, but they never show up over here. That's not usually the case when you live in a resort town."

Our whole group nodded in agreement. Those of us who live in a lively town—one with beaches, hiking trails, snowmobiles, great restaurants, theater, and other things that attract visitors—well, we sometimes find that we're everyone's favorite friend or relative.

Old college pals, childhood friends, and relatives as far away as third cousins once removed show up and ask if our guest rooms are available. We learn to lie unless we really want to see those people, and we shamelessly recommend motels and B and B accommodations to old college roommates.

"Of course," I said, "Dolly's mom is an invalid."

"I guess that's it," Lindy said. "Dolly goes there, but the sister never comes here. Although in the emergency her sister got free to come pretty quickly."

"She must have left around four in the morning," I said.

Joe chuckled. "You gals are sure suspicious."

"And not very charitable," I said.

We waited for the new arrival to emerge. It must have been about fifteen minutes later when Hogan, Aunt Nettie, and the tall red-haired woman came out. The woman—who must be Molly—was clutching Hogan's arm with one hand and mopping her eyes with a tissue in the other hand.

"It's simply awful to see Dolly like that," she said. Her voice seemed to break. "She's always such a bundle of energy."

"There, there," Aunt Nettie said. Or something like that. She seemed uncomfortable. I guess anyone would be, comforting a strange woman about a grievously injured relative, though Aunt Nettie can handle that sort of situation better than most can.

They walked toward us. As I had already seen, Molly had brilliant red hair much the same color as Dolly's. She was tall, but not as tall as Dolly's six foot two. And while Dolly was husky, Molly was on the skinny side. Dolly was covered with freckles, too, while Molly had that dead white skin that sometimes accompanies red hair.

The two of them were very different, I thought. Despite their hair, they didn't look as if they were even related.

Hogan and Aunt Nettie introduced Molly around. Molly Jefferson. Yes, she was from Clinton, she told us. Yes, that was near Detroit, several hours across the state. No, she'd never been to Warner Pier before.

"Of course," she said, "Dolly came over to Clinton frequently to see Mom."

Aunt Nettie offered to take her to the hospital cafeteria for some breakfast. Molly declined. Hogan offered coffee from the waiting room's urn. Another refusal.

"The doctor says they're going to ship Dolly off to Grand Rapids to see a specialist soon," Molly said. "She'll go by helicopter, but I guess I'll drive up there."

"You ought to rest awhile," Aunt Nettie said. "You can come to our house."

Molly sighed a deep sigh. "Right now I'll settle for a ladies' room," she said.

Aunt Nettie escorted her in the right direction. Lindy leaned over and whispered in my ear. "Molly sure seems familiar."

I murmured back. "She seems familiar to me, too. But why would she say she's never been in Warner Pier, if she has been? Could we have seen pictures of her?"

"I don't think so. Dolly never displays snapshots unless they show a new dessert."

"I'll try to talk to her."

Lindy nodded. "Maybe she'll fess up."

"Maybe she and Dolly quarreled or something. Look! Hogan is back. He might know something."

I quickly moved to a spot beside Hogan. "Molly

seems really familiar to both Lindy and me. But she says she's never been in Warner Pier before."

"So?"

"It just seems odd."

"Molly and Dolly both have red hair. And they're both tall."

"Yes, but . . ."

"What are you thinking? That Molly is some sort of fraud?"

"That seems awfully far-fetched, Hogan."

"If it will make you feel better, I'll call her driver's license photo up on the state system."

"I hate to ask you to do that." Actually I was eager for him to do it. I did feel uneasy and suspicious about this woman. And after Dolly had been attacked, we had to assume that she was in real danger.

I looked at Hogan closely. "But maybe an ID check would be a good precaution."

Hogan laughed. "I'll get Char to run one." Charlotte Dumphrey was his personal assistant. Like every such person, she actually ran the day-to-day operations of his department.

Shortly after that someone called Hogan back to the treatment area again. Aunt Nettie and Molly went along. Then the rest of us moved outside to a spot that overlooked the helipad that all hospitals are apparently required to have these days.

A hidden portal from somewhere inside the hospital opened and a gurney came out, followed by the appropriate personnel, plus Hogan, Aunt Nettie, and Molly.

The ritual of loading Dolly aboard a helicopter ambulance was carried out. Then Hogan, Aunt Nettie, and Molly were escorted over to the observation area, joining the rest of us. We all watched as the helicopter took off, whoop-whoop-whooping into the clear morning air.

Then some of us went back to Warner Pier, and the rest went to breakfast at the closest IHOP. Over pancakes Molly and Hogan reviewed the route to the hospital sixty-plus miles away in Grand Rapids.

"You turn onto eleven," Hogan said.

"Do you mean twenty-one?" Molly asked.

Hogan agreed that twenty-one was right, and I knew that it was. I wondered how Molly knew the correct route, if she wasn't familiar with our end of the state. But she was the one with the map. Maybe she was simply reading it.

After breakfast, we all waved her off. Then I grabbed Hogan. "Listen," I said, "this Molly. How did she know about the highways in Grand Rapids?"

Hogan growled. "Lee! It's okay! Will you let go of this? Honestly!"

Then he walked away.

But Lindy turned up in his place. "So Hogan thinks our suspicions are crazy," she said.

"I guess he's got better things to worry about."

"Maybe so, but I keep getting a flashback about this woman. I keep picturing her in an odd outfit."

"What do you mean, odd?"

"Well, with her hair piled on top of her head. And feathers stuck in it."

"Feathers?"

Lindy nodded firmly. "Feathers, Lee. Feathers. Purple feathers."

Chapter 14

Purple feathers? I pictured a feathered barrette or some similar geegaw used in the hair. But purple?

Why on earth would a red-haired woman wear purple feathers? She'd have to be color-blind.

Maybe that was harsh. An expert decorator or fashion consultant can blend any colors, just by picking the right shades. Purple, red, fuchsia, teal blue, banana yellow, and puke green. Mixing them up correctly does the trick, especially if the wearer is looking for a dramatic effect.

But when I saw Molly, she had not been dressed dramatically. She'd been wearing rust brown slacks, a khaki jacket, and an off-white cap. It looked fine, but it was conservative in both design and color. And these were perfect colors for a redhead, just the shades my high school fashion arts teacher would have recommended.

No, Lindy had to be wrong about seeing Molly in Warner Pier wearing purple feathers in her hair.

I climbed into Joe's truck, and we went home. On the way I called the shop. I was pleased when Bunny answered the phone because it meant she was taking some initiative. Until then she had stared at a ringing telephone as if it were going to explode if she put a hand on it.

Bunny said there were no current crises at TenHuis Chocolade, so I told her either Aunt Nettie or I would be in before the day was over. But not right away.

Then I fell asleep until we got home, leaving Joe to try to stay awake on his own. He's pretty good at that. I tell him it's because he's a natural athlete. He says it's caffeine. He had had a lot of coffee at breakfast.

Anyway, we staggered into the house and slept until about three o'clock. Then I got up and went to the office, leaving Joe in bed.

Bunny said things had continued to go smoothly during the rest of the day. Aunt Nettie had called in with instructions on keeping the chocolates moving with both her and Dolly gone. Her crew is expert, and this had worked.

When I arrived everybody was curious, so they gathered round, and I repeated the latest report that we'd had from Hogan. That didn't answer all the questions of Dolly's coworkers, so I made notes of the other things they wanted to know.

I assured the group that Dolly appeared to be improving, but she was to have no visitors. In fact, I admitted I didn't know for sure which Grand Rapids hospital she was in.

"Frankly," I said, "I don't know if this is because of her health or because law enforcement is demanding it. After all, Dolly was attacked by someone. And this happened only a couple of days after we had a killing on our premises. So they may just be keeping her under wraps."

Everyone looked worried, and most of them nodded. I went on. "So, if any of you have even a small hint of who might have wanted to hurt Dolly—well, for heaven's sake, tell Hogan or some other law enforcement official!"

The group broke up then, and I went to my office, ready to check my messages. I was still upset about Dolly. I sat down at the desk, but instead of checking messages, I picked up a random piece of paper and stared at it, trying to hide the fact that my mind was racing, but I was doing nothing. How could something this bad have happened to Dolly? My brave words about law enforcement keeping her under wraps were meaningless. The lack of information scared me; I was afraid she was going to die.

I thought back to the most recent time I had talked to Dolly. She had been worried, and in typical Dolly style, she wasn't worried about herself. No, she'd been worried about a friend. She had said she felt obligated to talk to her friend—what had she said?

"Before I squeal." Then she had oinked like a pig.

What on earth had Dolly meant by that? Had she merely been joking, as I had thought at the time? I had not associated her concern for her unidentified friend with the death of Abigail Birdsong. No, neither Dolly nor any friend she was likely to have could be concerned with that.

Could they?

I mulled it over, and an idea binged into being. Joe. He could give me advice. There's no sense in being married to a very smart lawyer if you don't exploit his professional expertise, experience, and common sense. In this case especially, his experience.

As if in answer to my mulling, the phone rang. It was Joe. "Hey," he said. "I'm finally out of bed. How about pizza tonight?"

"Sounds great."

"I'll order, if you'll pick it up on your way home."

"Deal. I think there's half a package of romaine in the refrigerator."

"Ideal deal. I'll make salad. Call me when you're leaving the office. Love you." The phone clicked off.

I'd ask Joe's advice as soon as I got home.

I picked up my messages, really looking at them this time, but a voice interrupted me.

Bunny was standing in the doorway. "Lee," she said timidly, "may I talk to you a minute?"

"Sure." I tried to turn my sigh into a yawn. "Come on in. I wanted to tell you what a good job you did today."

"Oh, thanks. I was just so worried about Dolly that . . . Well, anyway, I wanted to ask your advice."

"My advice isn't up to par. But ask away."

Bunny stared at her hands and twisted them together. "You know Friday night—the night Abigail was killed?"

"Sure."

"Well, I was down here in the evening, trying to do work I should have done in the afternoon, and I saw her get out of her car. She was parked right in front of the shop and the shade in the front door was up."

"And you tried to duck her. I don't think anybody can blame you."

"She didn't come here first, Lee."

"Where'd she go?"

"She went up the street, to Warner River Wine, or the store beyond it. Or I think she did."

"At seven o'clock? Was it open?"

"I don't know. She didn't go in."

"How do you know, Bunny? We can't see the front of that store from the front of our store."

"I had to peek through the gap around the shade in the farthest window. She was standing out by the curb."

"It would give you an odd angle."

"It did." Bunny nodded vigorously. "Abigail didn't go up close to any window. She just stood out by the curb and looked toward it. Then she made a little gesture, turned back this way, and came to the window in the door. She—you know . . ." Bunny demonstrated, cupping her hands around her eyes.

"You're saying that she tried to see inside this shop."

"Right. I mean, the lights were on here, so it was logical for her to try to see inside."

Bunny hung her head. "I just didn't want to talk to her. So I hid. Maybe if I'd done something different . . . anything . . ."

I interrupted to assure Bunny that there was nothing she could have done that would have helped Abigail.

Was there? I had no idea, but there was no use in Bunny beating herself up over what might have been. That's useless, as I learned a long time ago.

Then I changed the subject. "Why would Abigail have been interested in the wine shop? Was she a regular customer?"

"Heavens, no! Abigail was a complete teetotaler."

"I suppose Andrew Hartley was working there."

"I wouldn't know. He would have been if anyone

was. But I don't think the shop is open in the evening very often. Not this time of the year."

We ended the conversation with my usual admonition. "Talk to Hogan. He needs to know about everybody who was downtown that evening. Don't speculate to me. Tell Hogan."

At least Bunny didn't reply with, "Oh, I wouldn't want to get anybody in trouble" or "It's probably not important." I hoped she was beginning to see that she was in real danger of being arrested, and to understand that she needed to try to protect herself.

As I began to gather up my jacket, boots, and cap, I did ask her one question.

"By the way, what church does Andrew attend? Or do you know?"

"I know which one he went to when he and Anya first showed up in Warner Pier. But I'm not sure of the name. It's that small, independent church out on the bypass. Why?"

"Oh, at the hospital he said he would make sure that Dolly got at the head of their prayer list. To be honest, judging by his sister, I was a little surprised to learn he had access to a prayer list."

"I'm surprised, too, considering how Anya has acted over Beau. But that's not Andrew's fault, I guess. And churches are supposedly for sinners." She smiled. "I guess I ought to drop in."

I headed home. I had parked in front of TenHuis, and as I went out, Chayslee's front door—between the Clown Building and the wine shop—caught my eye. I swung toward it and rang the doorbell. There was a noise over my head, and I realized that windows were opening—both regular and storm windows. Chayslee's head came out.

"Hi, Lee," she said. "What can I do for you?"

"I just wondered if you'd heard those cats in the Dumpster again."

"There was so much excitement in this block last night that there could have been a gun battle and Mary and I wouldn't have noticed."

"I guess so. Sorry I asked."

Chayslee laughed. "Police cars, ambulances. And you've got a pretty good pair of lungs on you."

We both laughed for a minute, and then I spoke. "I'm glad to hear that I caught your attention. I'll try not to disturb you tonight."

"Oh, you won't. I'm spending the night at Mary's. We're locking this place up and taking off."

"I think that's a good idea."

"Anyway, the admin woman from the police department called and said they'd have a car around all night. Though I don't think there will be any residents staying here. Andrew said he's going to Anya and Beau's."

So he'd be in Bunny's former home. I wondered how Bunny felt about the house she'd shared with Beau being occupied by his new girlfriend and her brother.

"How many apartments in this block have tenants?" I asked.

"Just three that I know of. Dolly, Andrew Hartley, and me. This time of the year."

Chayslee and I waved, and she closed her windows.

Chapter 15

Only three apartments were occupied in our block. Dolly's, Chayslee's, and Andrew's. Interesting. Had any of those people seen anything?

How about the opposite side of the street? Did I know anyone who lived over there? Would they have seen anything?

Butt out, I told myself sternly. Hogan and the state police detectives would have quizzed everyone who might possibly have been a witness. I'd better keep my nose out of it, or I'd be in trouble anyway.

But somehow my thoughts about Dolly's neighbors—or lack of neighbors—had reminded me of our last talk. Dolly had been concerned about a misunderstanding with a friend.

Neighbor. Friend. In this case did one equal the other?

I picked up the pizza and went home for dinner. Joe

had salad and iced tea ready. As a Texan, I drink iced tea all around the calendar, and I've converted Joe to my habit.

But I was still thinking about those apartments. As I shook extra Parmesan onto my pepperoni I reminded Joe about Dolly's comments, about the last conversation she and I had before she was attacked.

"Did Hogan ask you about this?" Joe asked.

"No. He asked me all about finding her as she was being attacked. He didn't ask about the last thing she said to me. So I didn't tell him. But, Joe, Dolly laughed it off. She made the whole thing sound like a joke. I never thought about it being important."

"Still . . ." Joe pulled a slice of pepperoni off his pizza and nibbled it thoughtfully. "Still, Lee, you probably ought to tell Hogan."

"I guess I could write him a note and leave it at the station."

"Or call him. Tonight."

"Really?"

"It might be important. Didn't you ever make a serious comment and pass it off as a joke?"

"Well, sure. That usually results in hurt feelings. It means I'm saying something that later I'll wish I hadn't said."

"I'll remember that."

"It might be better for our marriage if you forgot it. But if I give Hogan some information, maybe I could get some."

"Like what?"

"Oh, like maybe alibis. Just because I'm nosy. I'd love to know where everyone claims to have been Friday night. And last night, for that matter."

"That would be interesting." Joe finished his slice

of pizza, then picked up the phone. "All Hogan can do is tell us to get lost."

It took a couple of calls to locate Hogan, and when we found him, he didn't sound at all glad to hear from us. Even though Joe did the calling. They are close friends, but with Joe defending someone Hogan was considering arresting—well, it was potentially awkward.

Joe handed the phone off to me, and I repeated the comments Dolly had made. Hogan was noncommittal, which was the attitude I'd been expecting.

"Okay," I said, "may I ask *you* a question now?"

"I may not answer."

"That wouldn't be a first. I was just wondering about alibis."

"Whose?"

"After you eliminate Bunny . . ."

"As you and Joe have."

"Right. She's completely out of it as far as we're concerned. Our nominees for most-obvious killers would be Beau and Anya. So, where do they say they were?"

There was a moment of silence. Then Hogan laughed. "I like the way you put that. Not 'Where were they?' but 'Where do they say they were?'"

"Oh, Hogan! They're just so obnoxious. You can't blame me . . ."

"I get it, Lee. I think Beau's been telling his alibi all over town, so it's no secret. Beau said they went over to Augusta Friday night. They ate dinner there. They spent the night at a B and B, fooled around visiting antique shops Saturday, stayed over again, and didn't come home until Sunday night."

Of course, that matched what Anya told me. "They may have been dodging Abigail," I said.

"Could be. Then last night, when Dolly was attacked, Beau says they went into Holland for dinner and didn't get back until late."

"Hmmm."

"Hmmm? Did you hear something different?"

"Not really. Andrew said he spent the evening with them last night. They are his alibi. Maybe he just meant he stayed at their house."

"We'll ask him. And we're checking with the Augusta B and B." There was a long silence. Then Hogan spoke. "Well, thanks for the tip. On Dolly and her friend. And if you hear anything more about Anya and Beau's travels, let me know." Hogan hung up.

Joe, naturally, had been listening on speakerphone. Now he punched the cell off. We looked at each other.

"Have we been given permission to detect?" I asked. "Hogan rarely tells me anything as direct as that 'if you hear' comment."

"I'd feel a little more comfortable if he'd added one of his usual caveats. You know, the one reminding you that there's a killer on the loose around here."

A rabbit ran over my grave, and I shivered. "Are the doors locked?" I asked.

The next morning I awoke determined to actually do some work at TenHuis. I hit the floor running. By eight thirty I had run the gossip gauntlet at the post office and was sitting at my desk.

Only then did I call to check on Dolly. Char, Hogan's secretary, had been appointed information central on her condition. Dolly had a good night, Char said. Her sister was still with her, but Dolly wasn't awake enough to say much yet. The doctors, she said, were encouraged.

Char gave a deep sigh. "I wish I could make a recording of all this," she said. "You know, 'press one for an update on the condition of Dolly Jolly.' But Hogan wants to know who calls."

"Oh? Well, who has called?"

"I probably shouldn't tell, but since it's you . . . Mostly friends and neighbors." She read off a list of a dozen people. None of them surprising. Mostly the people who had come to the hospital.

Then she added a comment. "Only one person I didn't know. Someone named Mike Westerly. His voice sounded gruff."

"Mike?"

"Who is Mike?"

"One of the construction workers on our remodeling job."

"Do I scent romance?"

"I doubt it." I thought sadly of the conversation that Joe and I had about Dolly's slim chances at romance. "I think she's been showing him around the building or something."

We hung up. But Char had made me curious. Why had Mike called? He'd come to the hospital, too. Again, why?

The mention of Mike took my curiosity in a different direction. To our remodeling project. When could it resume? Or had it already done so? Were the workers back on the job?

I walked back into our workroom. The door between us and the remodeling project was still tightly locked. But when I put my head out the back door, I was pleased and delighted to see activity in the Clown Building. Several workmen were going in and out.

One of them was Jack VanSickle, the contractor. I trotted after him.

"Morning, Jack," I said. "I'm glad they've let y'all start working again."

"Yep. I'd like to finish this job sometime, and we've hardly made a start."

"Yes, we don't want next summer's tourists climbing over sawhorses." Talk about joking when things weren't really funny? Was I doing that?

"May I look around?" I asked.

"Sure. Let me get you a hard hat," Jack said. "Actually I'm glad you're here. We need someone to look at the shelving in the basement, to see if it's deep enough."

"I'll get a jacket. And I'll see if Aunt Nettie will take a look. That's really her department."

I went back to my office for a jacket, plus a pad and pencil. Then I took my flashlight from my purse and stuck that into my pocket. I looked for Aunt Nettie, but she hadn't come in yet, so I stopped to measure the shelving in our current storeroom. One foot from front to back. Eighteen inches high. I wrote the dimensions on a sticky note and put it in my pocket.

When I got back to the Clown Building, I accepted an orange hat from Jack. He turned to talk to a worker, but I was now properly equipped, and I went toward the basement of the Clown Building on my own.

I come from a part of the country where basements are rarely found, so I find Michigan's underpinnings interesting. Here almost every building has a basement.

And they come in different styles. Our house—built around 1900—has what's known as a "Michigan basement." That's a basement with stone or cement walls and a sand floor. I've never been able to discover why it's named for our state. And no one has ever answered my big question: If a basement of that style is built in

Indiana, Iowa, or Wisconsin, is it still a Michigan basement?

But the Clown Building has a more standard basement, with cement walls and floor. In its day it had had some sort of plumbing and apparently some built-in cupboards and closets. Jack and his crew had pulled all of those out. They had repaired the walls and floor. The last time I'd seen it, the area had been bare of—well, anything. No storage shelves, no closets or cupboards, no light fixtures. Just bare walls and floor.

Jack VanSickle had not reappeared, so I stood on the stairs and began to look around by flashlight. I pictured how it would look when everything was built the way Aunt Nettie and I had planned.

The narrow stairway, for example, would be wider. It would also turn a corner so it could be longer. This would make it much less steep.

Instead of being made of old, creaky boards, it would have wider treads. The treads would be covered in a nonskid material. The result, or so we hoped, would be a gently sloping stairway, making it easy to carry boxes of tax records and crates of gift boxes up and down. Nearly all foodstuffs would be stored upstairs.

I found the notepad and pencil I'd stuck in my pocket. It took a lot of juggling to find a place for the flashlight while I made a note to ask about keeping insects out. Permanently. As in forever.

I was sure the workmen had improvised lighting of some sort in the basement, but I wasn't sure how to turn it on, so I used my flashlight as I started down the stairs. I assured myself that Jack would be down soon.

I clung to the handrail, made of plain old two-by-fours. Some light was coming from behind me, but going down the stairs was like descending into hell. I couldn't remember any natural light source—such as windows—in the cellar. Dark. Really dark.

I stopped four steps from the bottom of the stairs. Should I go back up and wait for Jack? As if answering my question, the door at the top of the steps blew shut with a bang. I jumped all over, and I probably should have gone back upstairs right then.

Instead I shot the light from the flashlight around. My purse was only equipped with a small light designed to help put a key in a keyhole or maybe find a dropped coin. Its beam was fairly powerful—thanks to the invention of LED bulbs—but it didn't illuminate a very large area.

I wasn't ready to retreat, however. I kept shining the flashlight around the big room, trying to get an idea of what was down there. The light bounced off a large stack of wallboard and a heap of steel rods—studs for future partitions, I guessed. It paused on a primitive table, the kind construction crews knock together out of scrap lumber. A small circular saw was on the floor under it.

There were other things. The floor was too cluttered to walk over with just my small flashlight. It would probably be a good idea to go back up and wait for Jack, I told myself. I could do nothing here.

The basement seemed to be a dead zone. Nothing moved, nothing breathed or wiggled or lit up or fell down or made a noise.

Until someone coughed.

The sound might as well have been an explosion. I jumped all over. And I dropped my flashlight.

I resisted the temptation to let out a loud swearword and flailed around with the hand that had been clutching the stairway's railing. That got me a barked knuckle, but I now had an idea of where the railing was. I felt around more gently and was able to grab it.

It seemed to be a lifeline. If worse came to worst, I could hold on to it and get up the stairs. If I did that, I hoped the door at the top would open.

I turned my attention to the sound that had startled me. The cough.

It had come from across the room. And now I heard dragging footsteps. And, yes, there was a light. It was feeble, but it was a light. The cougher wasn't an eyeless monster. It was a human being who used a flashlight to guide himself.

Keeping hold of the railing, I stepped back toward the basement's outside wall. I remember thanking God for my long arms. I was able to get next to the wall and still hang on to the railing. I stepped up a step, gently, trying not to make a noise, although whoever was in the basement must have seen my flashlight earlier and probably had heard me coming down the stairs.

For some reason, I didn't want to make a noise. Looking back, I have no idea why not. The only people in the building should have been construction workers. I wasn't afraid of them. Was I?

Anyway, step by quiet step I made my way up the stairs. One step. Another step. A third.

I managed four steps before I found the blankety-blank flashlight.

I stepped on it, of course. And it rolled, and I fell to my knees, and I screeched the word I'd been repressing.

Immediately the cougher's flashlight swung around and hit me with a light that seemed as bright as a Broadway spot.

"Hey!" The cougher's steps changed from dragging to rapid, and he came near.

Of course, the person was just an indistinct blob. But he was an enormous indistinct blob. I swung my fanny onto the step and looked toward the approaching figure, shading my eyes from the glare of the flashlight.

"Who is it?" I asked.

"It's just me," a deep voice said.

The blob aimed its light on its face. Since the light came from under the chin and was casting shadows upward, it made the figure more monstrous than before. But its action showed goodwill. I braced myself for danger, but I also hoped for the best.

"I can't see you," I said.

The light flashed around. "It's just Mike, Mike Westerly. I was going to come over later and ask you about Dolly."

And at that moment the door at the top of the stairs opened, and the basement was suddenly flooded with light.

Chapter 16

Jack VanSickle stood on the top step, staring down at Mike and me.

"What are you two doing down there in the dark?" he asked.

I tried to stop huddling against the basement wall and regain some dignity. "I don't know what Mike is doing," I said. "I'm trying not to feel like a foal. I mean, a fool! I fell on the step."

Continuing my idiot act, I moved my foot. I kicked my flashlight, and it fell off the step where it had landed. It bounced down the stairs, fell through the space at their back, then rolled underneath them.

"I didn't know where the light switch was," I said.

Proving that he was more intelligent—or perhaps more poised—than I was, Mike Westerly didn't try to explain himself. He simply grunted and turned away.

"Actually," Jack said, "you must have turned the

light off when you came through the door. It's kind of tricky."

"I wasn't down here in the dark," Mike said. "The light went off all of a sudden, and someone was fooling with a flashlight."

"I guess that was me," I said. "Sorry. Jack, what did you want me to look at down here? Some sheep? I mean, shelves?"

Gradually we straightened the scene out. Like a gentleman, Mike crawled under the stairway, found my flashlight, and handed it to me. I thanked him. Jack came on down the stairs, then led me over to some rough framing in a corner. This, he said, would become one of the main storage cupboards. Reading from the note I'd made upstairs, I described the size of the current shelving. I twisted my tongue only one more time, turning "gallon buckets" to "galosh buckles." I didn't even try to repeat it correctly.

Mike went back to doing whatever he'd been doing when I destroyed his routine. Now and then he eyed me, frowning.

Now that I got a good look at him, I realized he wasn't monstrous. Not scary like the figure who had loomed up in the dark basement. No, he was just a really tall guy, six-four or even six-five, with hair that stuck up every which way, blunt features, a chin firmer than John Wayne's, and a build like a bale of hay. One of the big round bales.

But when he had approached in the dark, with his flashlight casting crazy shadows—I would have been happy to nominate him for an award for Best Actor in a Horror Film. My imagination had run away with me completely.

Jack and I toured the basement, discussing which

sections of storage could be used for foodstuffs—those must be built of special materials—and which for non-food items such as molds, bowls, and shipping boxes. Then we headed for the stairway. Halfway up, I paused. I could see Mike over at the worktable, and I called to him.

"Mike, were you going to ask me a question?"

He growled his answer. "I'll do it later."

Jack and I went on up the stairs. As we moved out into the first floor, he grinned at me. "I hope Mike didn't scare you."

"He was perfectly polite and helpful." I didn't answer his question directly. Yes, Mike had scared the something or other out of me.

"I've never seen him do anything he shouldn't, but he is big."

"I'm big, too, Jack. Five-eleven and a half." I didn't point out that I was about three inches taller than Jack was. "My husband is six-two and my dad is six-four. I'm not intimidated by big men. Mike did sort of loom up in the gloom down there, and I stumbled on the step. He startled me, and I imagine I startled him."

"Mike seems to be afraid of women."

"Why?"

"Because he *is* so big, I guess. I think he does scare a lot of them." Jack grinned even more widely. "The only one he seems confident with is that Ms. Jolly."

"Dolly?"

"Is that her first name? She's kinda like Mike, I guess. So big that people are—well, a little afraid of her."

"Dolly is big. But she's one of the nicest people I've ever known. I can't imagine anyone being afraid of her."

I asked about the remodeling, then went back to the shop with my mind filled with question marks.

Was Mike just a friend to Dolly? Was that why he was asking about her all the time? Or was he the "friend" she had mentioned, the one she didn't want to "squeal" on?

I was careful not to mention what Jack had said about Mike and Dolly to anyone around the office. I did decide to tell Hogan, when I had a chance.

It was nearly lunchtime when Mike phoned me. "Miz Woodyard, I'm sorry if I scared you this morning."

"It was fine, Mike. With the nutty lights, I didn't recognize who you were. I'm sorry if I reacted sort of strangely. But you said you had a question."

"Well, it's Dolly. Miz Jolly. I called that number they were giving out, but all the news I got was—well, just kinda general information."

"Yes. That line was set up by the police, and that's all they can do."

"Yeah, I get it. But I thought you might know more. How is she really doing?"

"Mike, they're not telling me anything more than what you already heard."

"Oh."

"But if she was getting worse, I think they'd announce it."

"Do you know where she is?"

"No, I don't know that either."

"I thought I'd send her, you know, some—well, a card or something."

"I'm sure she'd like that, Mike. If I hear anything about her . . ."

I stopped talking. What more could I say? I wasn't going to promise that I'd tell Mike where Dolly was. In fact, I was sure I wasn't going to do that.

I stumbled on. "Anyway, Mike. I'll tell you anything I can."

Which wouldn't be much. I wrote Mike's cell number down and hung up.

It was an interesting situation. Was Mike interested in Dolly romantically? As a friend? Or was he her attacker? After all, it seemed as if the attacker would have to be a big man. And Mike sure fit the bill on that front.

His questions had also made me wonder again about where Dolly was. Hogan had been so careful not to mention which hospital she was being moved to, for example. He'd had a case a year earlier in which a murder attempt was made in a hospital. He knew it's easy to find a patient who's confined to bed.

That was one reason I hadn't done any active looking for Dolly. Finding her might endanger her. And I still found Mike pretty frightening. He might well be the person who attacked Dolly.

Although the person who had chased me hadn't seemed particularly big. But it's hard to judge the size of someone who's chasing you.

I decided to add Mike to my suspect list. Then Bunny came in to ask me a question, and I realized that list was fairly long.

There were my favorite suspects—Beau and Anya. Plus, let's not leave off Anya's brother, Andrew. They might not have any reason to harm Dolly, but they had plenty of reasons to kill Beau's aunt Abigail—if they hadn't known that she'd already changed her will to leave everything to Bunny. And there was no reason that they should know that.

The problem with those people as suspects, of course, was that whoever killed Abigail needed to be able to get into our building and into the Clown Building. And there was no reason to think any of those three could have done that.

The keys were important to the crime. Unless the killer knew how to get hold of the keys, he or she was unlikely to be able to get from one building to the other without leaving clues—such as tools used to break locks or other evidence.

And if they didn't have keys to Dolly's back stairway, then the whole crime was off. Because the detectives seemed to feel certain that the lock hadn't been jimmied.

Besides Beau, Anya, and Andrew, all the construction workers on the remodeling project were suspects. They had access to keys—both Jack's keys and, possibly, Aunt Nettie's and mine.

In fact, someone from TenHuis Chocolade was a lot more likely to have killed Abigail than Beau, Anya, or Andrew. The only person at TenHuis who admitted she hated Abigail, of course, was Janie. She was just a young girl! I had trouble picturing her as a murderer. But it certainly wasn't impossible.

Bah. Humbug. I brushed Janie aside as a suspect. But it seemed impossible that such a disreputable pair as Beau and Anya had no motive for killing Dolly.

Or perhaps I should say, no *apparent* motive. Could there be something that either of them was concealing?

But the most obvious motive for an attack on Dolly was that someone thought Dolly had seen something that linked the guilty party to Abigail's death.

I had felt sure that Abigail's will, or the threat to make such a will, was the motive for her death. But, heck, there were a million other reasons for killing people.

Revenge, for example. I recalled the story that Janie had told me. According to that, Abigail had ruined her father's livelihood by starting gossip, calling his honesty into question. If that were true, Janie's whole family could be suspects.

Abigail could have had other types of questionable business dealings. And as a gossip, she could have started other vicious stories harming other Warner Pier people.

She could have done almost anything, I told myself. And it was not up to me to figure it out.

Being nosy, I told myself sternly, was no excuse to speculate and ask questions about the guilt or innocence of my neighbors.

But I sure was curious about some of them.

Who's Who of Chocolate

COENRAAD VAN HOUTEN

In 1828 Dutch chemist and manufacturer Van Houten brought chocolate making into the modern age. He invented cocoa.

Van Houten worked for at least thirteen years to come up with a new process that produced powdered cocoa with low, low fat content. Van Houten invented "Dutching" and made the candy bar possible.

The process of making chocolate—from bean to solid—involves a long series of steps. One of the final steps is the grinding process. This ends with chocolate that's about 53 percent cacao butter.

Van Houten developed a new hydraulic press that reduced the cacao butter to 27 or 28 percent. This leaves a cake that can be made into a fine powder. Voilà! Cocoa was born.

To further refine the product, Van Houten used alkaline salts to help the cocoa mix well with warm water. This also made the product darker in color and milder in flavor. So when you buy cocoa, check the label. If it's "Dutched," it's thanks to Coenraad.

Chapter 17

Curiosity won over character. I called Bunny in and asked her a bunch of nosy—extra nosy—questions about Beau, about Anya, and about Andrew. Yes, she told me, Beau's full name was Edward Beau Birdsong. Yes, Anya was a correct name, not a nickname. And Andrew was twelve years older than Anya. His middle initial was *H*. She didn't know what it stood for.

That night after dinner I headed for the Internet. There had to be some information about my three favorite suspects out there someplace. And I hoped it was scandalous.

I started with Beau, since he would probably be pretty easy. Bunny had told me he was originally from a small town in Illinois, he had studied art in Chicago, and he was thirty-five years old.

I never ran into a duller person. Beau had not been sued for sexual harassment. He had not flunked out of any college I could find mentioned. He had never done anything. Anything. Except paint these cotton-pickin' bright-colored gigantic flowers. To me they looked like Georgia O'Keeffe rip-offs.

Beau had been born in Stamps Center, Illinois, and had graduated from high school there. The local weekly ran pictures of all the graduates—just the way Warner Pier's paper does—and the only honor listed under Beau's shot was "Senior Art Award." I already knew that he was an artist, of sorts. It ended with "Future Educational Plans: Chicago Art School." I almost expected it to say, "Aunt Abigail Scholarship."

The weekly ran a story when he and Bunny were married; both would have been in their early twenties. Bunny was from Chicago. Her parents were listed as "the late" Mr. and Mrs. Henry Culpepper. Obituaries for Beau's parents ran soon after the wedding notice.

Well, the young couple hadn't had much of a start. Neither of them had any immediate family, and they were joining a profession that usually required the help of a day job to get by. Maybe they had needed a boost from Aunt Abigail then.

A few other odds and ends had appeared in the hometown paper. Beau and Bunny had apparently lived in Chicago, but Beau had gone back to his hometown to present an art class for the middle school career day. Bunny had taught a class in art appreciation for the home ec club. The story identified her as a graphic artist. There were a few one-paragraph stories when Beau won prizes at various shows. None of them sounded very prominent.

I grew up in a small town, and I understood small-town life. Beau's life was absolutely predictable. I could have written up what I found out before I read the articles. I yawned as I moved on to Anya and Andrew.

Bunny had told me those two were from another small town, this time in Texas. That surprised me; neither of them had what I'd call a Texas accent. Oh, they dropped the occasional "y'all" into the conversation, but it takes a nasal quality in the voice to be a real Texan, and neither of them had it. When I typed in "art" and "Texas" and "Anya Hartley," however, I saw what was going on. Anya was identified as from Plano. To a person from Chicago, like Bunny, Plano might sound like a small town. We Dallasites know it as a wealthy suburb.

People who live there usually don't have strong Texas accents.

First, a suburb like Plano attracts "new Texans." People who have moved to Texas from elsewhere. And elsewhere may be anyplace from Texarkana, Arkansas—180 miles away—to New York City—1,500 miles away. Or even Dubai, Sydney, or the Shetland Islands. People in Plano associate with lots of non-Texans.

So lots of Dallas natives don't "y'all" at all, and they often use their noses for breathing, rather than talking through. When I first moved to Dallas at age sixteen, all the other kids made fun of my nasal small-town accent. I worked hard to get rid of it. I've never quite succeeded.

As for Anya, naturally there was much less information online for her than I had found in Beau's hometown weekly, where a PTA meeting is worth a news story. There was a Plano newspaper running articles about the locals, however, and I did find some items there.

Anya had gone to Plano West High School. She had been active in the art program, and the Plano newspaper had listed prizes she had won. I was able to find Web pages of some of the community art organizations and spotted Anya listed among exhibitors at their events. If she had gone to college or taken any other advanced art courses, no notice had appeared in the newspapers.

I thought I'd drawn a blank until one more "Anya Hartley" notice popped up. This turned out to be in the Plano crime news.

It was headlined "Stolen Car Crashes," and it had appeared ten years earlier. "Anya Hartley, age 25" had been driving a Cadillac SUV on Independence Avenue when it hit a light pole. Hartley was uninjured, and she flunked a DUI test. She was held for investigation when the vehicle proved to belong, not to her, but to a prominent Plano businessman. The businessman was found unconscious and uninjured in the backseat of the wrecked vehicle.

By the next day, however, the affair was sorted out a bit, and Anya managed to dodge a DUI charge.

The story didn't explain exactly how she managed that. However, reading between the lines, I decided that the prominent businessman had been too drunk to drive, and Anya had volunteered to take him wherever he wanted to go. However, she wasn't in tip-top shape herself, and they ended up embracing the light pole. I hoped that he paid her lawyer.

This led me to the *Dallas Morning News* files, where a few more items on Anya Hartley turned up. It appeared that she'd been quite a party girl in Dallas. Especially in the art scene.

I even found a picture of her taken at an art show

opening. The opening had a Grecian theme, and she was wearing a classically styled gown that showed plenty of cleavage. Her hair was in an upsweep, with ribbons wound through it. I couldn't see her feet, but I was willing to bet they were adorned with jeweled sandals.

Nowhere in these files, however, did I find any reference to Andrew Hartley. But why should I? A brother twelve years older would probably not be involved in his sister's social life. Besides, there was no reason to think that Andrew had lived in Plano, or even in the Dallas area, just because his sister did. But I tried him. "Andrew," "Plano," and "Hartley." The combination got thirty hits, but none of them was for an "Andrew Hartley."

No, it looked as if Andrew had gotten the heck out of Texas at a young age.

I sat and stared at the computer screen. I wasn't about to try Andrew Hartley nationally. That way lay madness. There must be hundreds of people with those names in some combination.

Then, on a hunch, I typed in "Anya," "daughter," and "Plano." Maybe Anya's parents were listed somehow, even if it was in the obituaries.

To my delight, an article came up. And it was an obituary. (Sorry about your demise, Mr. or Mrs. Hartley, but thanks for giving your daughter an unusual name.)

Again, it was the Plano suburban paper. Published eight years earlier, it reported that George Hartley had died. He had been born in Shawnee, Oklahoma, and had lived most of his life in the Dallas area, working as an advertising salesman. His wife of forty-five years, Yvonne, had died the previous year. Services were to be at the funeral home chapel at two o'clock the next day with the pastor of some mission presiding. Survivors included a daughter, Anya Hartley, and a sister, Constance May Kimball.

I stared at the obituary. I read it again. I got up and got a glass of water, drank it, and went through the whole process one more time.

Yep. That's what it said.

Then I yelled. "Joe! Anya Hartley is an only child. She doesn't have a brother!"

I think he'd been napping. Anyway, he was startled, and it took a lot of "huh's," "wha's," and "surely not's" before he joined me at the computer to check it out.

And neither of us was able to find any connection between Anya and Andrew Hartley.

"Of course," Joe said finally, "there are a lot of explanations. He could be a half brother."

"Yes, but if they have the same last name, there ought to be a parent named Hartley connecting them. And here we have a parent named Hartley, but no connection. At least it's worth looking into."

"Right. And Hogan may have already done that."

I nodded. "Should we assume that he has? Or should we mention it to Hogan?"

"Oh, I don't think it would hurt to mention it."

"Actually I could look around the Internet a bit more."

"Trying what?"

"Andrew is an artist. He has his little carved birds on display in the wine shop. He must have been in art shows someplace."

"Good idea."

I was pleased that Joe thought it was a good idea, but it didn't turn out to be terribly productive. I tried "carved birds," "art show," and "Andrew," figuring that people who change their identities tend to keep their first names. Maybe. It took a dozen tries before I came up with something.

And then I found an "Andrew Hartley" who had no connection to Warner Pier. Without the Texas bits, there he was.

Andrew Hartley had won third prize in an art competition in Arkansas three years earlier. Encouraged, I kept trying, and that time I came up with a Hart Andrews who had placed high in a show in Tennessee.

Ha! Hart Andrews. A whole new set of art shows. I kept at it. An hour went by. I looked at art shows, at art festivals, at folk art, at carvings, at birds, and finally I came up with an art show prize that went to "Hart Andrews, Mount Ida, Arkansas."

And there were pictures with it.

Unfortunately, Hart Andrews wasn't in any of them. But one of his birds rated a close-up. And the style, the colors, and the intricate carving were identical to the tiny, delicate birds that Andrew displayed in the Warner River Wine Shop.

I also got the name of the organization that sponsored the show. I was able to find their Web page—including a phone number. I should be able to call someone the next day. They might know something.

"You'd better talk to Hogan first," Joe said. "He may know all this, and you might even be busting up some big plan he has."

I agreed. So I planned to call him first thing the next morning. But at eight a.m., before I could call Hogan, I made another startling phone call.

I hadn't left for the office yet when Bunny called me. She had gone to the office early and had found a message from Stella Drumm. Yes, Stella. The buyer for a major department store. Stella sometimes gave me a royal pain, true, but the previous week she had ordered a ginormous number of Easter bunnies.

I assured Bunny that I'd call Stella immediately, and I actually picked up my telephone to do it. Using the contacts file, I punched the number. A muffled voice answered the phone.

"Hi," I said. "Do you need more Easter bunnies?"

There was a pause. Then the voice on the phone became clearer.

"Lee? Is that you?"

I realized that instead of Stella Drumm, I had called Dolly Jolly. And Dolly had answered.

Chapter 18

"Oh gosh!" I don't know if I whispered or yelled. "Dolly, I didn't mean to call you! I intended to call Stella Drumm. I guess Dolly and Drumm are right together in my contacts. How are you?"

"Oh, I'm doing pretty well!" Dolly sounded okay; at least her voice was booming. "I'm feeling much better, and they're going to let me take a shower today! How are things at TenHuis?"

"We miss you, but we're limping along. I know you aren't supposed to have visitors."

"I know, and I'm bored silly! Hogan comes by once a day, and that's all the visitors I can have! I think there's a sign on my door saying I'm contagious! And I can only watch so much television!"

"When Hogan comes, you ask him if you're allowed to have phone calls. I called you accidentally, and my name may now be mud."

"All he's interested in is something he says I told

you about knowing a secret! Lee, I can't remember anything about that!"

I tried to make my voice soothing. "Do you remember who was coming for coffee at your place that evening?"

"No! The last thing I remember is Thursday night, way before the time he says I was attacked! It all just fades out after that! It seems as if I was going to tell Hogan something, but I can't remember what it was!"

"I guess that's typical of a concussion. And you're entitled to a concussion." I shut up without mentioning the pipe the attacker had been swinging. I didn't want to give Dolly nightmares.

"It sure is frustrating!" Dolly gave a deep sigh. "I'm racking my brain!"

"Stop racking it and just relax." I gave a sigh that matched hers. "I'd better stop talking to you. If Hogan finds out I called, he'll hide you in a new place."

"I didn't know I was hidden! I'm just sitting here, bored silly! This sister they've got with me doesn't even play gin rummy!"

"If you just can't stand it, call me. But if you don't recognize the voice that answers, hang up! Don't blow your cover!"

Dolly boomed good-bye, and I ended the call with my heart pounding.

So my guess—not even a serious guess, just an idle musing—had been correct. Hogan was keeping Dolly under cover. Literally under cover. In a hospital bed. With nobody but her sister with her.

I couldn't tell anybody. Well, maybe Joe. I could whisper it in his ear when we had our heads under our own covers tonight. But if it got out, it might— what? Endanger Dolly? That was obvious. It also might let her attacker escape. And that attacker was also probably the killer of Abigail Birdsong.

Obviously this was some plan of Hogan's. He had gone to a lot of trouble to keep Dolly hidden. I didn't want to be the person who blew the secret.

In fact, I didn't even know the secret. I hadn't asked Dolly what hospital she was in.

That made me laugh, at myself, and I was giggling when I called Stella. Luckily, Stella didn't need anything serious. Then I headed for the office.

The first thing I did was talk to Bunny. I was still supposed to be teaching her the ropes on the electronic side of TenHuis Chocolade. And for the past two days I'd almost ignored her. My conscience was giving me guilty twinges.

All was going pretty well, Bunny reported. She had a few questions on the online orders, and we hashed those out. But she still seemed pretty down.

"How are things going for you?" I asked. "We haven't talked for the past couple of days. I've been remiss."

"Oh, I'm kind of blue. I talked to one of Abigail's closest friends this morning. She had just heard about her death. It was a sad call."

"Grim. Is this someone here in Warner Pier?"

"No, someone in her hometown, Stamps Center, Illinois."

"I forget that Abigail didn't even live here most of the year."

"I know. Abigail used to call Beau, but I rarely talked to her during the winter. This Maxine—that's the friend, Maxine Robb—called me wanting to know about the funeral."

"Has it been set?"

"Apparently not. I called Beau to ask, and he gave me some vague answer. I keep telling Maxine to call Beau, but now that she's found out we're separated, she doesn't want to talk to him."

"I've been thinking I should do you a favor of some sort, Bunny. So give me the phone number for Maxine Robb. I'll call the funeral home—since we have only one in Warner Pier, that will be simple. Then I'll call Maxine Robb and give her an up-to-date report."

The relief on Bunny's face gave my spirits a lift. So I called the funeral home and was told that no services had been scheduled yet for Abigail Birdsong, but they expected an announcement the next day. I deduced that Beau was supposed to make arrangements that afternoon or evening.

Then I punched in the number Bunny had given me for Maxine Robb.

A breathy little voice answered. "Bunny?"

"No, this is Lee Woodyard. I work with Bunny."

"Don't tell me something has happened to *her* now."

"Oh no. Bunny is fine. She's just needed to get some work done, and I said I'd call you to report on the plans for Abigail's services."

"Oh?"

"And the report is—no report. I think Beau is to visit the funeral home to make arrangements tonight."

The breathy voice gave a breathy sigh. "Oh drat! That's what comes of leaving it to Beau. Bunny would have had everything arranged by now."

I realized she was right. Despite her sometimes inept behavior, Bunny did get things done. As long as it wasn't something that required grace and agility.

I gave an artificial laugh. "Well, I'm afraid Bunny is out of the loop for the moment, at least as far as

Abigail is concerned. And, of course, they had to have time for the autopsy. I'm sorry we can't tell you more."

"It's very frustrating. If the funeral is on Saturday . . . But Beau and the new bimbo may come up with something crazy."

"Is there a Birdsong family plot there at Stamps Center?"

"Oh yes. Abigail's brother—Beau's dad—is buried there. But I'm positive there isn't a plot up there at Warner Pier, even though the family spent a lot of time there. But the Birdsongs were a pioneer family here."

This was the same town where Beau had grown up. Maybe I could get a little information from Maxine. "Beau grew up there, didn't he?"

"Oh yes. Abigail was so proud of him. All his artistic accomplishments."

"Has the Birdsong family always been artistic?"

"Not at all! Of course, they were loaded. Owned thousands of acres of central Illinois." Maxine giggled. "And not a little Illinois Central."

I tried for a friendly chuckle. "Good investors, then?"

"Abigail's father was almost like the Wizard of Omaha, except he lived in Stamps Center. Everything the man touched turned to cash. But he was a regular philistine. And proud of it. You know the type."

"Not interested in culture?"

"Not at all! Abigail used to be embarrassed. He'd give money to any cause except the arts. And nothing to education except vocational programs. He dropped out of high school, you see. He was completely self-educated. Not stupid, you understand. He studied on his own. I guess Abigail inherited the state's largest collection of books on economics and the stock market. But the man had no civic spirit at all.

"With Abigail's strong interests in the arts and culture—well, he was a trial to her. And he wouldn't let Abigail travel. Wouldn't let her go to college. Simply sat on her. Her brother—Beau's dad—he was like the father, except he lost money instead of making it. She longed for something to feed the spirit. Art. I guess that's why she tried so hard to encourage Beau."

Maxine gave a little sniff. "It's just so sad for her to be the victim of this terrible crime right now."

"It's certainly a tragedy," I said. "But why especially now?"

"Didn't Bunny know about it?"

"If she does, she hasn't told me."

Maxine gave another of those sighs. "I guess it's no secret now. Abigail was about to be married."

Married? Abigail? I'm sure I gasped. A hundred comments and questions went through my brain. I had to clamp my jaw to keep them from flying out of my mouth. Saying something like, "Abigail! Married? Well, I'll be hornswoggled," wouldn't be at all tactful.

But I had to say something. "My goodness! Had she been married before?"

"No! It was all new to Abigail. If she hadn't told Bunny, then I expect I was the only person who knew about it."

"Who was she engaged to?"

"Oh, it wasn't official yet."

"How did she meet him?"

"They met at some meeting at the Field Museum. Abigail was a patron. A thousand-dollar giver."

"Wow! Of course, the Field is science, not art—but still . . ."

"Oh, this man was a big art supporter, besides his

interest in science. He was an artist. Had exhibited all over."

"What was his medium?"

"Medium?"

"Yes. Was he a painter? A sculptor?"

"Oh! Well, I know he painted. And maybe sculpted, too."

"Did she have any of his work?"

"Just one piece. A little figurine. Of herself. He got her to pose for him. When they first met. I guess that's how they first got well acquainted."

"How romantic!"

"It was romantic. I guess any of us would be bowled right over by a man who created something like that for us."

"Golly! This is exciting! And it's so sad! I mean, that she died! And so tragically. Where did he live?"

"Up there in Michigan someplace. Not too far from where Abigail went every summer."

"Oh? We've got scads of artists up here."

"I know. That's why she liked it so well up there. She could go to art shows all the time, and there were plenty of people to talk to about art."

"I'm all agog! Who is it? What's his name?"

"Huh!" Maxine gave a snort. "That's where she got cagey."

"What do you mean?"

"She would never tell his name. Even to me."

Chapter 19

All the air rushed out of my whole being.

I could barely say good-bye to Maxine and get off the phone. In fact, I twisted my tongue into four knots at once trying to do it.

"Franks, Maxine, for tolling me. I really apprehend this information. It may be valiant."

"Huh?"

"Sorry," I said. "I'm famous for my mixed-up talk. I'll talk to you again soon."

I hung up. Then I held my head in my hands, feeling weak as a newborn Texas calf. And only part of my weakness was because of my twisted tongue. Yes, I'd mixed up my words. But that was nothing to the way I'd mixed up my whole view of Abigail and her world.

I'd regarded her only as a nosey parker, a pain in the neck trying to run the lives of her relatives. A conniver, maybe. A bossy old woman. An enabler for a dependent relative. Now I saw there was a lot more to Abigail's situation.

And I felt sorry for her. Sorry for a young woman brought up by a domineering father, one who "sat on her," as Maxine had said. Though she was a good student, and he had plenty of money, he wouldn't let her go to college. He scoffed at her artistic interests. He refused to allow her even to travel. She wanted a larger view of the world. Instead, he confined her to Stamps Center, Illinois.

And I had scoffed at her, too. When I considered possible motives for killing her, I had rejected romance. Because Abigail was not young and beautiful, I didn't even consider that she might have had a suitor, that someone might have liked her, even loved her.

Oh, I knew lots of plain women with loving husbands, but I thought they had caught the eye of those men when they were younger and more desirable. But for Abigail, romance had come late in life.

Or had it been real romance? Had Abigail been the target of a con artist of some sort? I considered that, but somehow I didn't see that happening to a person as no-nonsense as Abigail had been.

Had Abigail refused to tell her friends about her suitor because she was afraid they would laugh? That was certainly another possibility.

Whatever the rhyme or reason for Abigail's secrecy, it could be important to solving the mystery of her death.

I called Hogan. Naturally he wasn't at the police department. I left a message, describing my information as "important." Was it? I didn't know.

Then I trotted back to Bunny's tiny office, went in, and closed the door behind myself.

I took a deep breath and spoke. "Did you know that Abigail had a boyfriend?"

Bunny froze. "That sounds silly," she said.

She listened silently as I repeated what Maxine had told me. "Maxine said she didn't mention it to you because she thought you already knew," I said. "Did you?"

Bunny shook her head silently. "I had no idea." Tears welled in her eyes. "How terribly sad."

We both sat there, crying and feeling sorry for Abigail and maybe for all the other lonely women we knew. Not women who were independent, who had decided to rely on themselves. But women who longed for love and companionship and because of personality, appearance, or attitude were never going to find men who would want to give it to them. And who would hide their longings with all sorts of disguises—bossiness, avarice, hunger, sometimes even lust.

"Oh, Lee," Bunny said. "Am I going to become like Abigail?

I shook my pity off. "Not a chance!" I said. "You'll never be a harridan like Abigail. And now we both need to buck up and stop being foolish."

We both laughed a little, and I quizzed Bunny. Maxine thought she had been the only person to know about Abigail's boyfriend. And Bunny said she'd known nothing. But was there anyone who might have known?

Bunny said she couldn't think of anyone immediately. But she'd give it some thought.

"Of course, I'm out of touch with Stamps Center," she said. "At least Beau and I escaped that fate. Beau's dad wanted him to run the feed store." She shuddered.

"Why did all of you—Abigail, Beau, and you—think

of Stamps Center as a fate worse than—anything? I grew up in a small town. We live in a small town now. It's not so bad."

"There's a big difference between Stamps Center and Warner Pier, at least for the Birdsongs. The shadow of Beau's grandfather hangs over all of them. The town was fine for most people, but Beau and I tried living there for two years. It really was a nightmare. Believe me, Abigail was not all bad. She helped us escape."

"You know, Bunny, that interests me. Beau's family had such close ties with Stamps Center, but you two wanted to escape. And so did Abigail, in her own way. You all escaped to Warner Pier. So how did Warner Pier, Michigan, become part of the Birdsong picture?"

"The family story is that Beau's grandfather took the property here as payment for a bad debt. I expect he planned to sell it, but he never did. Maybe he'd sat on Abigail and on Beau's dad until he felt that he at least owed them a nice place for a vacation. And he died ten years after he acquired it. Then it passed to Abigail, and she probably liked the artsy connections."

I went back to my desk thinking about what a sad story this was. I tried to put it aside and work. But I kept picturing Abigail with a man. Who was that man? Where did he live? Did he have a day job? Would he show up to join the mourning for Abigail? Did Beau know him? Would he come to the funeral? Would anyone realize who he was? Was he handsome? Or plain? Could he be a rugged type, a sort of John Wayne with a paintbrush?

I realized that I had no idea what he looked like. I hadn't even thought to ask Maxine about his appearance. Or his age, for that matter.

I reached for the telephone and called her.

After a few explanations, I asked my question. Could she tell me anything about the age or physical appearance of Abigail's boyfriend?

"Well, once we did talk about how old he is," Maxine said. "She said he was a little younger than she was. Just a few years, she said."

"How old was Abigail?"

"She graduated a year ahead of me. So I guess she was sixty-one."

"I guess 'younger than she was' would be in his fifties?"

"Maybe even late forties. It's hard to guess. But she didn't seem to think people would be shocked because she had taken up with a younger man. Or an older man."

"Did she ever mention what he looked like?"

"She said he wasn't particularly good-looking. But he had lots of personality. Always joking. And very generous. He'd never allow her to pay if they went out."

"Sounds like a great guy."

I hung up and tried Hogan's number again. This time Char told me he was available.

But he didn't sound friendly when he came to the phone.

"Hi, Lee. What can I do for you?"

"This time I'm doing something for you, Hogan. I talked to a friend of Abigail Birdsong's, and did I pick up some info!" I quickly told Hogan what I had learned from Maxine.

"Hmmm." That was his only reply, but it was an interested "hmmm." When I offered Maxine's phone number, I could tell he was writing it down.

"And that's not all," I said. I quickly ran through the information I'd gleaned from the Internet on Anya.

I ended with Andrew not being listed as a survivor at Anya's mother's funeral.

That got another "hmmm."

"I expect you could ask around in the artsy circles here," I said.

"Yes, I could. But not you!" Hogan snapped the words at me. I knew I was going to get his regular lecture. "Now, listen, Lee. There's a murderer loose around here. You stay out of it. Your safety is in the bad guys not knowing that you know anything about the deal. You're already in some danger because you saw the guy."

Chapter 20

A ll I answered was, "Yes, sir."
This caused Hogan to hang up abruptly. When I get seriously respectful, he knows I don't mean it.

The next reaction, about ten minutes later, was a call from Joe. "What did you say to Hogan?" he asked. "I just got a really hot call from him. Complaining about you."

"I agreed with him in a truly respectful manner."

"No wonder he's mad. You're not about to do something silly, are you?"

"No, Joe. Seriously, I'm not. All I've been doing is looking around on the Internet. I found some interesting things, and I passed them on to Hogan. First he said they might be valuable, then he began to warn me off."

"He worries about you. What had you found out?"

I told him what Maxine had said about Abigail and her boyfriend.

"One of her best friends told me that," I said.

He gave a low whistle. "They have a serious shortage of personnel in law enforcement around here. All that stuff you learned certainly gives Hogan a few new lines of questioning, which is a help. But he gets afraid you'll get too involved."

"Joe, I really don't intend to do anything more. I was just curious about what's out there."

"Well, watch your step," Joe said. "Leave the questioning to Hogan."

I sat at my desk and tried to be a good girl for a while, pretending to be noncurious. Then Mike Westerly walked by my window. He was wearing his yellow hard hat and was headed into the Clown Building, ready to build something up or tear something down.

The sight of him was so tempting that I couldn't resist. I opened the Internet and looked up "Mike," "Westerly," and "construction." There were, of course, hundreds of things on the Internet that included those words. There were Westerly Construction companies in at least six states, for example. There were other companies that included the word "Mike" with completely unrelated words. "Mike Jones Insurance of Westerly, Alaska, specializing in construction projects" for example. But way down at the end was a reference to a carpenter's union in Detroit, Michigan.

And "Mike Westerly" was membership chair. Detroit. Aha. It sounded like our Mike. Dolly's fanboy.

I changed my search to "Mike Westerly Detroit." Thank goodness for suburban weeklies. Almost immediately I learned that Mike Westerly had graduated from high school twenty-five years earlier. He had received the technical department's award for furniture making.

After that things got harder. Was he the Mike Westerly who sang and played guitar with a local country and western group? How about the guy who entered the chili cook-off? Both of these were connected with Detroit.

The country and western group turned out to be easy. The group—The Lake Huron Five—had its own Web page. It hadn't been updated in ten years, but—once on the Internet, forever on the Internet. There was Mike, looking younger but just as rugged, clutching a guitar.

The chili cook-off was harder to trace. When I finally found a complete story about the chili-cooking Mike Westerly, he appeared to be younger than the one in Warner Pier. Plus he had moved to Detroit from Tennessee. He just didn't sound like a graduate of a Detroit high school.

I looked at one final entry—"Westerly wins design competition." It didn't sound like our rough, tough Mike.

But there he was, leaning over a gorgeous table that had a big blue ribbon hanging over the edge.

The table was an odd shape. I'd call it deliberately whopper-jawed. The finish looked like satin. There was inlay in a simple design. I can't describe it in artistic terms, but it was stunning. It had been selected for a prize of $1,000.

Again, Mike looked younger and not so rough-hewn. But it was definitely him.

"Who'da thunk it," I said aloud. "An artiste."

The only other Detroit listing I found for Mike Westerly was a divorce notice. Gee. Having been through a divorce myself, I knew how much potential for personal change there was in that situation.

That seemed to end the references to Mike Westerly. Of course, it wouldn't end the actual information that existed on Mike, only what I could find with a simple search of the Internet. And I'm not particularly expert on the Internet.

If I found the right people, however, there was a lot more to know about Mike Westerly. If Mike had moved in the artsy circles, for example, I could think of three different people in Warner Pier who were likely to know more. At least three people I knew worked in wood, were active in state arts circles, and would either know Mike or know people who knew him.

I resisted calling any of them. Hogan wouldn't like it, and as a rule I wanted to get along with Hogan. I did call Hogan and leave a voice message telling him he might find interesting information on Mike Westerly on the Internet.

I tried to pay attention to my own work for the rest of the day. I particularly avoided calling Dolly. But I thought about her. So maybe it was mental telepathy when she called me.

Her voice was booming as usual. "Hi, Lee!"

My voice was hushed. "Hey! Are you okay?"

"Of course. My jailor left the room for a few minutes, and I thought I'd like to hear a friendly voice!"

"I'm glad to make friendly noises at you, but did you get Hogan's permission to talk to me?"

"He hasn't been here today! It's been more boring than usual!"

"Boredom isn't going to kill you, young lady. You just take it. Unless you have something important to say, I'm hanging up."

"No! No! I had something to tell you!"

"What was it?"

"It's gone! It flitted away. But it was something about that back door!"

"Your back stairway? Is Hogan asking you about that?"

"Yes! But I don't remember anything!"

"Take a nap, Dolly. And the next time Hogan calls, ask him if you can call me. Okay?"

"You're more likely to see him!"

"Maybe. And if I do see him, I'll confess that we've been chatting and ask if it's all right. But he may take your phone away."

I hung up. And I tried to think about my own business for an hour, though my own business wasn't nearly as interesting as people getting killed and beaten up on my block.

But about four o'clock I saw a Warner Pier police car pull up in front of TenHuis Chocolade. The sign on the side door read CHIEF. I was hit by a wild thought that Hogan had come to arrest me for endangering one of his witnesses. Or at least to bawl me out. I almost panicked, but I'd calmed down by the time Hogan came into my office and dropped into my visitor's chair.

"Hi, Lee," he said. "I may owe you an apology."

"Why?"

"You called me with some valuable tips, and I told you to butt out."

"I know you don't like it . . ."

Hogan stopped me with a gesture. "No, you found out some important things. Now, I already had somebody working on the background of Anya, Beau, and Andrew. Bunny, as well, for that matter, and you didn't look her up. It hadn't occurred to me to add Mike Westerly to the list. What was his connection with either Dolly or Abigail?"

"I don't know of any connection with Abigail. But as for Dolly—well, he told me he wanted to send her a card. I was surprised to learn that he had that much interest in her. Then—Mike is such a big, husky guy, maybe kind of scary. The contractor, Jack VanSickle, told me that Mike is wary of women, probably because of his rough, tough appearance. But Jack said that Mike seemed to like Dolly. So I wondered about their relationship. It may be nothing."

Hogan frowned. "Yes, that raises questions. We're looking at his history."

"Anything there?"

"It's vague. When he and his wife were divorced, she complained that he threatened her and that he tried to cheat her over money."

"That's not good."

"No, it's not. But we don't know that it's true, either. People say a lot of things during a divorce. But the witness you dredged up who may be extremely valuable is that Maxine Robb."

"I didn't find her, Hogan. She popped up on her own. Bunny knows her."

"Yeah, you said she kept calling Bunny until Bunny didn't want to talk to her anymore."

"So I took on the chore, and here came all this information about Abigail having a boyfriend."

"Apparently Maxine was the only person Abigail Birdsong told about the big romance."

"But does that mean anything?"

"We don't know yet, but anything Abigail kept such a deep secret could be important. Char's working with the Michigan State Police to try to track down who the guy was. They had to appear in public together sometime. Someone must have seen them."

"How about Andrew? Is he really Anya's brother?"

"We haven't tracked that down either. But the two of them have presented themselves as brother and sister for at least five years. So it's not just a new thing. And, of course, there may be some explanation, like they're half siblings or something. And neither of them gave us any heartburn about letting us have their fingerprints. We're running the prints now, just in case."

"They're probably the most innocent people on the planet. And certainly Andrew is perfectly pleasant to know. But Anya is so unlikable—I'm probably prejudiced against her merely because she's obnoxious."

Hogan nodded. "On the other hand, Beau's life seems to be an open book. He's pretty much a jerk, of course. I can't help hoping Bunny gets to keep the money."

We both sat quietly for a few minutes. Then Hogan spoke. "But I keep losing sight of one of the main points here. The keys."

"Which keys?"

"All the keys, but especially the keys to the back stairway."

"So you still think that's where Abigail was killed."

"She may not have died there. But she must have been attacked there. The bloodstains."

"If she was killed over there, how did the attacker get her into the Clown Building?"

"I think he carried her through TenHuis, Lee. Pretty easy trip if he borrowed one of those rolling tables. They would have come in through that door that goes into your break room. Across the workroom. Through the door into the Clown Building."

Hogan stood up. "Have you counted up how many keys that trip took?"

After he left, I counted it up. Three keys. Or was it five? That's how many keys would be required to get from Dolly's apartment through TenHuis Chocolade and the Clown Building, then out of that building.

We really needed a system of keys that was more efficient, I thought. Also more secure. The current system was a mess. I vowed that we'd be installing a better system as part of our big expansion project. I wrote a note about that in big, fat letters on my memo pad.

Then I thought about our cumbersome system of keys and how many were needed to kill Abigail and move her body.

One key: opens outside door to Dolly's apartment. It could be the street door key, at the front of the building, or it could be the back door key, on the alley.

Second key: needed if Abigail came through the front. It opens the door from Dolly's kitchen into the back stairway. If Abigail had been inside Dolly's apartment, she would have had to start on her fatal path by going through that door.

Third key: opens door to our break room. There the killer could load Abigail's body onto one of our rolling carts and push her body through the break room, through the workroom, and over to the door between the two buildings.

Fourth key: would be used to open the heavy padlock that kept the temporary door between the two buildings locked. Abigail's body was then arranged near the back door. The cart was pushed back into the TenHuis side. Sawdust had been discovered near the adjoining door, although any tracks had been destroyed.

Fifth key: The killer—or killers—would have to get out into the alley. This might require a key to a door leading out of our building either from our break room or from the Clown Building. Or the killers could have gone out through the back stairway leading from Dolly's apartment to the alley.

Since all this had happened the night Dolly had been visiting her mother, Dolly would probably be unaware of the entire series of events.

But that wasn't really the point. The point was, how was Abigail enticed into that back hall? Or was she attacked elsewhere and dragged in there?

Compared to Abigail's murder, the attack on Dolly—three nights later—had been a snap. Her killer had apparently arranged to come by her apartment for coffee. He rang the front doorbell, and when she answered the door, he hit her with a pipe.

Only me and my key chain alarm had stopped him from finishing her off.

If Dolly ever remembered who was supposed to come for coffee . . . But so far she hadn't remembered. It could have been a dozen different people. It didn't even have to be a man. A woman could wield that heavy pipe.

It could have been someone she knew well, or someone she had barely met. It could have been Mike. And it could have been someone like me.

Or even someone like Bunny.

Who's Who in Chocolate

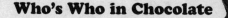

MILTON HERSHEY

Say "Hershey" to Americans, and they automatically answer "Kisses." Or maybe "Bar." This is a tribute to one of the world's marketing geniuses, Milton Hershey.

Hershey began life as a poor boy. At fifteen he began work in a confectionary in Lancaster, Pennsylvania. At nineteen, he had his own business manufacturing caramels. At the World's Columbian Exposition in Chicago in 1893, he saw chocolate machinery. At the end of the exposition, he bought the machinery, then sold his caramel business for a million dollars. He used the money to buy a farm in Pennsylvania and started a chocolate factory.

There he also built an ideal city for his workers. Fire station, library, home for boys, five churches, a hospital, schools, hotels, golf courses—and a roller coaster. His own cows produced milk for his chocolate; his own plantations in Cuba contributed sugar.

Today in addition to enormous chocolate sales, Hershey's Chocolate World theme park draws huge crowds every year.

Chapter 21

Joe and I had both denied Bunny could be involved.
Why had we done that?

Because we were extremely naive? I didn't really think we were.

Joe, in particular, had spent a few years as a defense lawyer. In general he tends to be rather doubtful of his clients' innocence. The way our legal system works requires that he defend his clients whether he believes they're innocent or guilty. What he thinks about it doesn't matter.

However, in Bunny's case Joe sincerely believed she had had a rough deal in life, but had kept her basically sweet nature. He did not think she was likely to kill anyone.

I hadn't known Bunny until Joe recommended her for a job. But after working with her for three months, I would have described her—not me—as the naive

person. She was completely unsuspecting. The kind
of person the other kids sent on a snipe hunt.

Her husband, Beau, had an affair; she didn't tumble
to what was going on. Beau talked her into giving up
her own art; she meekly accepted his statements that she
had little talent. His aunt kept telling her that Beau was
brilliant; Bunny joined in the worship at his shrine. Aunt
Abigail ordered her around; Bunny gave in, never doubt-
ing that Auntie knew best and trying to keep the peace.

Of course, it was possible that Bunny had finally
realized that Auntie didn't always know best. She
might have rebelled and let Auntie have it with a blunt
instrument. Certainly I would have done that; I am far
less patient than Bunny is.

As for the attack on Dolly—well, Dolly would certainly have been willing to let Bunny into her apartment. She liked Bunny and, as I did, wanted to give
Bunny every chance. If she'd had a suspicion about
Bunny, she would have called Bunny and asked her to
explain before she called the police. An action that was
almost fatal.

Yes, Bunny seemed naive and unsuspicious. Was
she really? Or was it all an act?

I sat at my desk and sighed. Forget it, I told myself.
If it's an act, it's a good one. You're committed to believ-
ing in Bunny. I sighed again and looked out our front
window. What I saw there led me to have a temper
tantrum.

Bunny was walking up to our street door arm in
arm with Beau.

"Yah!" I didn't yell, but I made a loud, disgusted noise.

I leaped to my feet. What on earth was Bunny doing? What was Beau doing? What was going on?

Could I throw myself on the floor and kick my feet? Could I curse? Scream? Hit someone? Who?

Bunny and Beau didn't come inside. They paused at our door, arm in arm, looking into each other's eyes and talking.

I wanted to throw something at them. Where could I find a rock when I needed one?

I wanted to shake Bunny. Instead I got up, grabbed my coat from the rack in my office, and headed out the back door. I had to calm down. I could not pitch a fit in front of the whole shop.

I walked down the alley, around the corner, and into the Sidewalk Café. Coffee. Coffee would be a temporary answer. Maybe caffeine would calm me. Or a soothing cup of tea.

The restaurant business was so slow at that time of the afternoon that no hostess was on duty. I simply walked in and planted myself in the first chair at the first table I came to. It took a few minutes for the one waitress to offer to take my order. I asked for black coffee and a snickerdoodle. This was a departure for me; if sweets are available, I always go for brownies. But right then I wanted to get my brain as far away from chocolate as possible, to forget TenHuis. I sat there, still huddled in my winter coat and hat, and sulked. I even yanked my knitted cap down over my forehead. I pulled out my cell phone, stared at it, and pretended I wasn't me.

And it didn't do a bit of good. Warner Pier is simply too small a town. Especially in the winter. Everywhere you go, you always know someone.

My coffee had barely arrived when the street door opened, and I heard footsteps coming in. I ducked my head even farther, staring at my cell phone. The footsteps stopped at my table. I heard a man's voice.

"Lee? Is that you?"

It was Beau Birdsong. Biggest jerk on the planet. The person I was maddest at, standing right there, apparently wanting to talk to me.

There wasn't a darn thing for me to do but act gracious.

"Hello, Beau."

"Lee, I'm so glad to run across you. Can we talk for a moment?"

I waved my hand at the chair across from me, though I didn't speak.

Beau sat down. "Lee, I want to thank you for your kindness to Bunny. You've made all the difference to her during this difficult time."

"I haven't done anything I wouldn't do for any employee, Beau."

"You've really helped her, Lee."

I took a big slurp of my coffee and hoped he'd go away. But no such luck. No, Beau waved at the waitress and pointed at my coffee, apparently wanting his own cup.

I stayed quiet. If Beau wanted conversation, he was going to have to make it himself. But he didn't begin talking until his coffee had been delivered.

Then he dropped his head into his hands dramatically. "How do I get myself into these messes?"

I didn't answer, but merely picked up my cookie and took a bite. When Beau looked at me, I shrugged.

"Lee, I swear this thing with Anya started merely as a little flirtation. And now Bunny and I are in this major legal situation. How did it happen?"

I decided I didn't have the patience to discuss Beau's problems. I ate the last bite of my cookie, slurped my final swallow of coffee, and stood up.

"Sorry, Beau," I said. "You have to figure out your own problems. So long."

I headed for the door, then turned back. "I'm sticking you with the check," I said.

I was rude. I didn't even feel ashamed. I walked back to my office ready to whack Beau. How did he have the nerve to dump Bunny, then do a contrition act?

The possibility that he might really be contrite flitted through my mind, but I rejected it. He had treated my friend Bunny badly, and that's all I cared about.

I went into TenHuis ready to skin anyone who spoke to me. And the poor sucker who came into my office first happened to be Bunny.

"I had a question about one of the e-mail orders," she said. "I'm afraid it needs to be handled today."

I answered her curtly. "What is it?"

"It's that Stella Drumm," she said. "Does she get the special discount?"

I assured her that Stella got practically anything she wanted. "She's in the top ten percent of our customers," I said.

Then I took a deep breath and asked the question that had been burning in my mind.

"What were you and Beau up to this afternoon? I was surprised to see you together."

Bunny sighed deeply. "Oh, Lee, he's such a baby. He asked me to go along and decide some of the plans about Abigail's funeral."

"Anya isn't helpful?"

"I think Anya wants to shove Abigail in a hole. And Anya knows nothing about small-town funeral customs. I guess someone is going to have to go down to Stamps Center and pick something for Abigail to wear, talk to the minister, pick the hymns, and everything else."

"Can you shove it off on Maxine?"

"I don't think so. Maxine hasn't been to church since 'Nearer, My God, to Thee' was popular. And I happen to know that Abigail hated that hymn. So I may be stuck. The worst part is, I'll have to drive down with Beau."

"With him? In what capacity?"

"Ex-wife, I guess. I'm sure not going as spouse. But he's invited me to ride down with him. The problem is that I don't have a car. So it's hard to turn down a ride."

"Can you make the plans on the phone?"

"A lot of them. But I'll still feel guilty if I don't show up for the service."

Bunny stared at the pen she held in her hand. "You know, I used to resent Beau because I had to wait on him hand and foot. Now I see that I wasn't doing him any favors."

"How so?"

"I took care of things for so many years that now, in the little everyday stuff, he can't make a decision. He doesn't seem to know what to order for lunch, for example. He doesn't know what to wear, how to pay the bills, when to—come in out of the rain! He may be a great artist, but he's just not competent!"

"Bunny, don't let him talk you into deciding all those things again."

"Oh, Lee!" She shook her head. "I believe I'm past that point. He'll have to learn to take care of himself. Or let Anya help him!"

I made a pencil into a miniature baton and twirled it with my fingers. "Am I to understand that Beau came to see you today, asked you to help him with the funeral plans, then told you—or demonstrated—how helpless he is without you?"

"I guess that's pretty much it. He made me feel sorry for him."

I waited a minute, twirling my pencil, before I spoke again. "Bunny, has it occurred to you that Beau uses this helplessness to manipulate people?"

"Oh yes. His dithering around gets so tiresome! It just gets easier to do it yourself than to wait for him to make a decision."

"Today—did it occur to you to ask Hogan, or Abigail's lawyer or someone, if Beau found out about the change in her will?"

Bunny drew her breath in sharply. "Oh, Lee! That would explain it, wouldn't it? I'll bet he found out last night."

Then she looked at the ceiling. "That bastard!"

Then she got up and went back to her office, leaving me feeling much better about her. I also felt better about my display of temper when I was talking to Beau over coffee. He had simply been trying to manipulate me.

Beau was still the biggest jerk in Warner County. Maybe the world.

Bunny's epiphany about Beau allowed me to buck up and do some work. I was hard at it when everyone, including Bunny, went home. Joe had spent the day at his Holland office, so I called and told him he was on his own for dinner.

"I've simply wasted too much time today," I said. "I'll have a truffle or two and keep working."

"I might take my mom out to eat," he said. "I haven't talked to her lately."

"Don't rat me out as a neglectful wife."

"You're not neglectful in the more meaningful aspects of marriage. Love you, kid. Don't be too late."

I hung up with a nice warm feeling in my innards. I'd really picked a good guy this time.

With that encouraging note, I waved cheerfully at everyone going out the door. I heard all the workmen leaving the Clown Building, and I made sure the padlock on the temporary door between the two buildings was locked.

Alone in the shop, I chose a couple of truffles from the reject piles in the back. When I needed sustenance, I could choose a Candy Cane truffle ("white chocolate filling enrobed with dark chocolate and trimmed with a pink and green X") or an Amaretto truffle ("milk chocolate filling flavored with almond liqueur, then enrobed with milk chocolate, and trimmed with chopped almonds").

The Candy Cane truffles were left over from Christmas, and therefore had been tossed into the "forget it" pile. I could eat as many of them as I wanted and not feel guilty. Greedy, maybe, but not guilty.

I made sure all the doors were locked, closed the shades on the show windows, and settled down at the computer.

It was an hour later that I heard a door open in the back.

Chapter 22

My first thought was that Aunt Nettie had come back for something. After all, in theory only three people have keys to that back door—Aunt Nettie, Dolly, and me.

So I called out. "Aunt Nettie!"

And no one answered.

That was the moment I got uneasy, maybe even scared. But I told myself to calm down. Probably I was mistaken about hearing the door.

Use the standard cure for odd noises, I told myself. Go look.

If there's nothing there—and there won't be—forget it. People who live in houses built in 1904 are thoroughly familiar with that cure because we hear lots of strange noises, and they all have to do with wood shrinking and expanding. So I left my office and went to the door to the workroom.

The retail shop, just off the street, was brightly lit.

Since it adjoined my glass-walled office, I had lights on in both areas. But when I looked into the workroom, I was looking into a pit of darkness.

I reached around the doorjamb into the workroom, felt for the light switches, and flipped the main switch. The workroom was flooded with light.

And there was nothing there that shouldn't be.

The workroom is twenty-five by fifty feet. There's nothing mysterious about its contents.

From the retail shop's door I could see all the stainless steel worktables, now turned askew because mopping the floor had been the last thing the chocolate ladies had done before they left. The tables rolled unless the wheels had been locked into place, and because of the mopping this hadn't been done. So the tables were every which way.

Along the sides of the room were the rolling racks used to move trays of chocolates, the storage cabinets, the sinks, the chocolate vats—one each for white, milk, and dark—the giant commercial refrigerator, and the big gas stove. The copper kettle on its stand-alone gas heater, waiting for Aunt Nettie to apply her magic to a batch of ganache, stood in a corner.

There was nothing there that shouldn't be. I didn't think there was even anything missing. It was just right.

I asked myself why that silly noise had made me so nervous. I had spent hundreds of hours alone in this place without being nervous.

It was probably something to do with TenHuis becoming a murder scene.

I continued my advice to self. *So, look around, Lee. Check the break room, the restrooms, the locker room, the pantry. There is nothing here that shouldn't be.*

I used a firm step as I went back through the work-room and into the break room. I flipped every light switch I passed, illuminating the whole place even more.

I looked behind Aunt Nettie's desk, stuck in the corner of the break room until our expansion was completed. I even looked under the desk.

Then I turned to the locker room and the restrooms. They were the hardest areas for a nervous gal to face.

The locker room isn't a room at all, actually. It's just an alcove off the break room with small lockers where the ladies can put their purses. Their coats hang on hooks on the back wall, with a flag mounted on a staff stored in the corner. We display the flag on holidays. I merely glanced at that area; with no employees work-ing that evening, only two abandoned raincoats were hanging on hooks near the flag, and a couple of pairs of boots were lined up in the corner. Everything there was just as usual.

The restroom was the only area enclosed by walls, and I did have to steel myself to look in there. There were only two stalls—the remodeled building would have four—and the stalls held nothing but plumbing equipment. I even looked in the storage closet. Nothing.

Then I checked the back door. Locked.

I felt relief flood my brain. I had looked everywhere, and there was no one. Nothing. Not a thing out of place. I gave the break room a final once-over and turned to go back to my office.

And somebody smothered a sneeze.

I couldn't believe it. A sneeze? I must be hearing things. Then three things happened.

First, I pivoted to see what was behind me.

Second, the flag fell on the floor.

Third, a person wearing black from head to toe jumped out of the corner where the flag had been. He was swinging something.

Fourth—yes, there was a fourth—I screamed a scream that curled the paint off the walls.

I should say I ran through the workroom, dodging worktables and other paraphernalia. But, no. I was simply too surprised. I kept standing there, screaming, for a beat too long.

The black-garbed figure was staggering around, trying to get clear of the flag and the raincoats. He stepped on the flagpole. It rolled, and the person skittered around, nearly losing his balance. He—I guessed it was a he—recovered and came toward me waving something like a broomstick, a short broomstick. And I shrieked another shriek before I took off for the front of the shop.

And what I was thinking was, "Why didn't I bring my cell phone?"

Because I hadn't. When I came back to check, I could have stuck it in my pocket, but no. I had left it on my desk.

So, to get away, I not only had to run through the workroom, dodging stainless steel tables. I also had to find the keys for the front door, open it, get outside, and run for the nearest human habitation. And at that time of the evening, no business was likely to be open closer than the Sidewalk Café. And the footing from here to there was slick.

Well, if I had to, I had to. I vowed to outrun this weird person. Period.

I knocked into one of the rolling tables, and my pathway widened. But that would help my pursuer.

So I whirled back, grabbed two of the tables and pushed them together, blocking the aisle.

And I kept screaming, though I had no idea how that would help. Neither Dolly nor Chayslee was in her apartment. Andrew? His apartment was two buildings away. Probably he was not within earshot. But I screamed again. And I once again pushed two tables together. And I ran for the front of the store.

And then I fell down.

I think I caught a foot on one of the wheels of those stainless steel tables. At any rate, I went sprawling, slowed my fall by grabbing a table, hit the cement floor, then slid along like an Ice Capades reject. I came to rest with my head in an enormous mixing bowl.

The lower shelves of all those tables are covered with cooking gear—big cooking gear designed for making large batches of bonbons and truffles. Mixing bowls, molds, and a whole lot of gadgets, thingamajigs, contraptions, and doohickeys were on the lower shelves of the tables.

I pulled my head out of the big bowl. I used one hand to grab a spoon a yard long and the other to scoop up the huge bowl. Then I leaped to my feet.

I whirled to face the person in black. He was still waving that wooden stick, sort of a miniature baseball bat.

He swung it at me. I waved my big metal spoon back at him and held the big bowl in front of myself like a shield. We sparred around like dueling musketeers.

The noise was terrific. Between steel hitting steel, wooden bat hitting steel, my screaming, the black figure roaring like an animal, stainless tables banging into each other—well, it was quite a clamor.

I guess we might have gone on for hours, if he—I was still assuming it was a he—hadn't slipped, exactly the way I had slipped earlier. Only he wound up sprawled on his back, across a bottom shelf. He knocked over a bowl that was full of small Easter molds—eggs, chicks, ducks, and baskets. What seemed like a million stainless things flew onto the floor, making a noise like dumping an Erector set onto a patio, only louder. Those molds bounced and clamored in all directions.

The black figure rolled over and tried to stand up. There were so many small things on the floor that he couldn't do it. He was still on his knees when I gave a table a hard shove and slammed the edge of it into his forehead. He collapsed backward, falling against the table behind him. That table, naturally enough, flew backward and rammed against the wall. The black figure lay there limply, his head resting on a gallon plastic jug.

I stood there panting. Thank goodness, I thought, we didn't knock the chocolate vats over.

Then I reached through the tangle, grasped the ski mask by its top, and pulled. It came off, and I saw the blond hair and handsome face of Beau Birdsong.

"You rat!" I said.

Then I ran for the phone.

Twenty minutes later the shop was a mass of people. The 9-1-1 call had gotten quick results. Hogan had been among the first there, along with Jerry Cherry and two other Warner Pier patrolmen. Michigan State Police, EMTs, Aunt Nettie, Joe—the gang was all there, and I had reached the stage of nervous talking.

"I guess we know who killed Abigail Birdsong and attacked Dolly," I said. "I always knew Beau was the biggest jerk in west Michigan, but he seemed so inept that I didn't seriously suspect him of killing his aunt. He's just not smart enough."

Hogan spoke in his usual quiet tone. "Well, it certainly looks as if Beau has been up to no good. But all we have on him right now is breaking and entering."

"But how did he get in?" Joe asked.

"He must have had a key," I said. "But how could he get one?"

Hogan shook his head. "There's no key on him."

"We'll have to search the place. He's ditched it somewhere," I said.

At that moment I saw that the EMTs were loading Beau onto a stretcher. Aunt Nettie and I had cleared the floor enough for people to walk in that area. Now we all stepped back to let the gurney roll past. I saw an ice pack on Beau's forehead, and I happily wished him two black eyes. I was so excited I was ready to chase him down again, gurney and all.

But as Beau went past, he looked up, giving that pitiful "Lee." His voice was pleading. "I never meant to hurt you. I only wanted to look around the shop for a scarf. I hid in the restroom until everyone left. But you never left! And the scarf wasn't where it was supposed to be."

Chapter 23

Once again displaying her desire to console people with food, Aunt Nettie took Joe and me to her house to eat the ultimate comfort meal: potato soup.

She collected potatoes, onions, carrots, and chicken broth, then cooked it into a soft mixture and mashed it. She thinned it with canned milk and butter until it was soup. We were sprinkling grated cheese, diced ham, and chopped green onions on top by the time I calmed down enough to ask a question.

"Won't it be awful if Beau really wasn't going to do anything bad?"

"Why would it be awful?" Joe asked. "He was definitely someplace where he had no business being."

"Yes, but I could have killed him when I shoved the edge of that table into his forehead."

"The EMTs thought he'd get away with a bad headache and a black eye. If I'd been there, he would now be tied in a clove hitch. And his knees would be attached to his shoulder bones."

For a second there Joe looked truly fierce. I paused with my spoon in midair. Gee. He really was my knight in shining armor.

"Thanks for the protection plan," I said. "But what was the scarf he was looking for?"

"Probably a red herring."

"And what was Anya yelling about outside?"

"That I heard," Aunt Nettie said. "She was throwing a real temper tantrum, screaming that Beau had an alibi."

"That may be right," I said. "I remember that she and Beau claimed they'd been over at Augusta when Abigail was killed. Hogan was checking it out."

"I think we can trust Hogan to check the alibis out thoroughly," Joe said. "But Beau has definitely blotted his copybook with this one."

I ate a spoonful of buttery potato soup. That stuff was more soothing than any prescription of tranquilizers known to medical science. Especially with soda crackers lightly topped with real butter. Yum. The world was looking better.

I shut up and ate. But my mind kept working. I mentally reviewed all those things I had found on the Internet—the information I had compiled on Beau, on Anya, on Andrew, and even on Mike Westerly. Was there anything in there that I had missed? Beau was definitely not going to admit quietly to his aunt's murder or to the attack on Dolly.

I vowed that I'd again take a good look at everything I'd found out.

Aunt Nettie plunked a dish of celery in the center of the table. Half of the celery was stuffed with pimento cheese and half with peanut butter. Joe and I both reached for a piece.

"Aunt Nettie, you're an angel," I said.

"Not yet," she said. "And as mad as I am tonight— that someone would attack you right there inside Ten-Huis Chocolade—I'm so furious that I may never make heaven!"

Soothed by people who loved me, I finished my dinner and went home to bed. But before I went back to my regular work, I would try to finish my ideas about researching Anya, Beau, Andrew, and Mike— the people I called "the suspects." The next morning I called the office and told Aunt Nettie I wouldn't be in until I finished some work at home.

I worked on my online research, beginning with Beau. Again, I found nothing that wasn't boring. Yawn.

Then I did the same thing with Anya. Same result. The big news with her was that Andrew didn't seem to be her brother, and I'd already figured that out.

On to Andrew. And that's when I remembered I had intended to find out more about the art show in which he had won a top prize. Again the Internet didn't let me down.

The Central Arkansas Nature Art Competition popped up again, with a link to the Web site. And there was the name of the executive director, Harriet Smith, followed by her phone number. I looked at my watch. Arkansas was in another time zone, but it wasn't too early to call.

Harriet Smith's voice took me right back to Texas. To a linguist, Arkansas and Texas don't sound alike, but Southern Country seems to be related to Southern Country, wherever it's from. And Harriet Smith's accent was definitely Southern Country.

I explained who I was, though not why I was calling, and told her I was trying to find out more about an artist named Andrew Hartley.

"He carves beautiful little birds," I said. "I noticed how close his name was to an artist who once won your show, Hart Andrews."

"Yes," Ms. Smith said. "Hart won our show about five years ago."

"Oh good! Then you remember him. I wondered if he had been using a pseudonym."

"Actually"—she drawled the word out—"I never met him, either as Hart or as Andrew. He was here a year or two before my time on the show's board. But I heard a lot about him."

"May I ask what you heard?"

"Is this for publication?"

I stretched my answer out as far as I could. "No. Ma'am. Maybe I'm just nosy. But we've had a serious crime up here, and I'm assisting the chief of police—who happens to be my uncle—in getting background information on witnesses."

"Witnesses? Then Andrew Hartley is not accused of anything?"

"Not at the moment." She was still silent, so I took the plunge and leveled with her. "Listen, Andrew may not have done anything at all. When you meet him, he seems like a very nice person. But . . ."

"Uh-huh."

"But it's hard for my uncle to ask for an official report from law enforcement in Arkansas if he doesn't have any real evidence. However, this Andrew keeps popping up."

"An official report wouldn't mean anything," Ms. Smith said. "There was no official investigation."

The two of us were silent. Then we spoke at once. I said, "I could get my uncle to call . . ."

She said, "I've been looking you up online as we talk. Tell me the name of the police chief."

"Hogan Jones."

"That's right. And you're all over the Internet, Mrs. Woodyard. Especially after being attacked last night. But the name of Andrew Hartley does not appear in this news story."

"I know. But his sister, Anya . . ."

"Anya? She was his niece when they were here. Is she mixed up in this?"

I explained how the victims and the people I suspected were involved. I ended with, "And except for Beau Birdsong—who attacked me last night—I don't really know of any evidence against them. Beau's aunt was the murder victim, but Beau doesn't seem to benefit from her death."

Harriet was silent, then spoke abruptly. "Lee, do you Skype?"

"Yes, I do, and I've got a fresh pot of coffee."

She laughed. "And I have got information and an opinion."

In a few minutes the two of us were having a nice chat over coffee and computers. Harriet was a sixtyish lady with gray hair in a long braid. A real artistic type. I liked her immediately.

"Just don't record any of this," Harriet said. "I'm about to break all sorts of slander laws. But I'm convinced that Hart Andrews caused grievous harm to a friend of mine."

"I can speak to my uncle off the record. He'll know how to use the information."

"I probably shouldn't say anything. But I will. I had

a close friend who was on the board of this organization. Shirley Church. She was a wealthy widow. She loved art, was an artist herself—watercolors. And she was devoted to this show. She had lots of money, and she solicited lots more donations from wealthy people in our area. Terrific gal."

"Every organization needs some of those."

"To an outsider, it seemed as if Shirley had everything. Money, friends, education, intelligence."

I pictured Abigail. "But was Shirley lonely?"

Harriet laughed bitterly. "None of us realized how lonely. She fell for this Hart in a big way."

"I'm sorry to hear that."

"The whole, well, affair was kept under wraps. He never asked her out until he moved on to another city. They would meet in Little Rock. She didn't confide in a soul here. I found out about it too late."

"Mmmm." I made what I hoped was a sympathetic noise. "I'm afraid I've heard this story."

"I'm sure it follows a pattern. After several months Shirley confided in me. She didn't tell me she had given money to Hart. No, she told me she'd made some foolish investments, and she admitted that she was quite depressed about it. In the end Shirley took an overdose of sleeping pills."

"How tragic!"

"She was afraid people would find out he'd conned her, and she just couldn't face it."

"Harriet, I'm so sorry to hear that. I suppose it wouldn't have helped for her to find out she wasn't the only one."

"The only one! Heck, she wasn't even close to the first one! We were able to trace Hart—who insisted on paying for all their dates and whom she had to beg to 'let her help him' with his investment crisis—well, we found where he'd been before. A couple of towns in Missouri. We found two other women with the same story! But nobody wanted to press charges! It was too humiliating. And in each case the man had used a different name! He was Hart Andrews here. In the other cities he'd been Harry Ambrose and Ambruster Hayworth."

Ambruster Hayworth. That sounded familiar, but I couldn't stop to figure out why. I kept talking. "I'm sure afraid that we have a new case here in Warner Pier. But how did you find out that Harry, Ambruster, and Hart were all the same person?"

"Oh, somebody is always taking pictures at these art festivals and shows. But sometimes you have to scrounge around to find them."

"If you've got pictures—well, I'd sure like to get a look at them."

"Our board wasn't able to take any action, of course. *We* hadn't lost money. Both the Missouri ladies involved asked us to keep it quiet."

"Then Hogan will have to go through official channels. If worse comes to worst, he might be able to get a warrant for those pictures."

Harriet was silent, then she sighed. "Maybe I can find a set in the files."

She didn't sound happy, so I tried to encourage her.

"Harriet, another person I believe was involved with Hartley-Hart-Harry-Ambruster-Andrew has been attacked. If he'd been charged earlier, maybe she would still be alive. Alive is better than embarrassed."

Harriet took a deep breath. "I'll find another set of those pictures if I have to paint one," she said.

She promised to call me back, or to call the Warner Pier Police Department if I wasn't available. We hung up.

For a moment I sat still, too wrung out to call Hogan.

We'd been looking in the wrong direction all the time. Abigail's will had nothing to do with her death. Beau may have tried to avoid being dropped as an heir, but that wasn't the reason his aunt had been killed.

She had died because she recognized Andrew. I even remembered the moment when it had happened.

They had come face-to-face in the retail shop of TenHuis Chocolade, just as Abigail had lashed out at Beau about his split with Bunny. Abigail had given a little gasp and stared at Andrew. Andrew had said something about the wine shop. Then he had said he would be there until it closed at nine o'clock.

I had spoken to him, if I remembered correctly. I had called him "Andrew."

Under what name had Abigail Birdsong known him?

It could be Ambruster, Harry, or Hart Andrews. It could be any of millions of other names. The man I knew as Andrew simply had to be the heartbreaker from Arkansas and Missouri.

Abigail had even written his name, Ambruster Hayworth, on the scratch paper she used as she wrote her will.

I had to tell Hogan this whole story.

A phone call to the police department was useless. Hogan wasn't there. All the delay did was force me to calm down and think quietly.

I had to have proof. And the proof was on its way. Harriet Smith was looking for the pictures of the artistic con man. She should have copies of them to me soon, maybe that morning.

I paced the floor. And as I paced, I tried to make the whole story fit together.

In my version, Anya and Andrew were con artists, working as partners. Sometimes Anya pretended to be Andrew's sister, sometimes she apparently took other roles—sister, artist, maybe partner in a gallery, niece, or just a friend. And if there was a man who needed to be conned, rather than a woman—well, Anya was in place and ready to entice him.

In my tale, Anya and Andrew worked art shows, identifying wealthy people in each community. By skipping across different regions and using aliases, they were able to hide their identities.

But in each community Andrew would make a play for a wealthy woman. Or maybe Anya would make a play for a wealthy man. In Warner Pier, they might have done both. In Andrew's case, at least, he would not accept money or assistance and would insist on paying for all dates and gifts. All meetings and dates would be held out of town, and Andrew would request that his ladylove keep their relationship secret.

What reason could he give? Whatever it was, it would probably exploit the pride of the woman who was his prey. She would not want her friends to know she was seeing someone, because the possibility of rejection was too real to her.

Each victim would be selected for two reasons. First, she had money. Second, she would be like Abigail Birdsong, a plain woman who was bossy, or perhaps shy.

And she was lonely. Even if she had plenty of women friends, she would be lonely.

I stood at the kitchen window and stared out at the bare trees in our yard. Why did my description seem familiar?

Dolly.

I nearly wept. The description I had given for Andrew's typical prey almost matched the one Joe and I had made when he and I were discussing Dolly several days before.

Dolly was a wonderful person, Joe and I had concluded. But she was not likely to be attractive to men.

Joe had smiled. "Men are shallow," he had said.

The only problem with my theory was that Dolly didn't have any money.

Chapter 24

Harriet's call didn't come until after ten o'clock. Then all she said was, "I'm e-mailing the photos."

The photos came before I could get the computer open. They were just snapshots. Harriet had also sent the name our guy had been using and the location where each photo had been taken.

"Hart Andrews—Central Arkansas Nature Show," the first one read. Next to it was a photo of a man grinning widely and holding a small knife. His head was turned to the left.

The man was definitely known in Warner Pier as Andrew Hartley.

The other two photos were easily recognized as Andrew Hartley as well, despite being identified as Ambruster Hayworth and Harry Ambrose.

I printed out five copies of each photo and of its caption, then called Harriet back. "You're a real crimefighter," I said. "Wonder Woman. I'm incredibly grateful to you, Harriet."

"If we can get the guy who hurt Shirley, I'll be happy," she said.

I gathered up all my files and stowed them in a manila folder. I called Hogan again. Again, he wasn't at the police department. I tried to tell Char about what I had found out, but I could tell that I was merely confusing her.

So I gave up. "Just tell Hogan I'm headed for his office," I said. "I have important evidence. *Important!* I'll try to be there very shortly."

And as I hung up I saw Andrew Hartley pull into our driveway.

I was thunderstruck. I don't think I've ever seen such a frightening sight. Knowing what I knew about him now, just seeing him on my property terrified me.

I grabbed the phone and once again called Char.

"I need a patrol car," I said. "I've got an intruder."

"What's this about, Lee?"

"Andrew Hartley just pulled into the driveway," I said. "I'm now convinced that he is the murderer of Abigail Birdsong and the attacker of Dolly Jolly. Please! Get somebody out here."

"Oh, all right," Char said, disgust in every syllable. "Since it's you. But you can't call the cops just because an acquaintance you don't want to see comes into your yard. You'd better have something to back this up, or Hogan is going to let me have it. And you, too!"

I was sure my doors and windows were locked, but most of our shades and curtains were open. If Andrew looked through a window, he could see me. I huddled in the bedroom, ducking into the closet. This gave me only a sliver to look through, but I was afraid to walk around the house and see what Andrew did. I was working purely by my sense of hearing.

As nearly as I could tell, Andrew did nothing but walk up to the doors and knock on them. Oh, I think he may have peered in the bedroom windows, but I was in the back of the closet with a very narrow view. Then I heard a motor start up and a van that looked like the one Andrew drove passed the windows, headed out. Although my car was parked in our drive, he must have thought I wasn't there.

Then I heard a siren, and in a few minutes Patrolman Jerry Cherry pulled up in the drive. I ran to the door to greet him.

I tried to explain what I had learned about Andrew and why he had frightened me, but like Char, Jerry merely looked puzzled. It was only a few minutes before he spoke.

"Listen, if you're okay, I'll run on. Hogan's gathering his forces for a big search of some sort."

"Just follow me out to the highway," I said. "I'd feel much safer with you behind me.

I gathered my belongings, including the five copies of pictures sent to me by Harriet. Then I drove to the police department. There I gave three of the copies to Char. As she looked at them, comparing the names and places on the backs, her face grew surprised.

"Oooh," she said. "I see why you were upset."

"Yes, and I'm going to be upset until Andrew—or whoever he really is—is behind bars."

With the information from Harriet delivered, I went on to the office. And was I sorry I did that. Anya was lying in wait inside the front door.

When I came in, she leaped to her feet, so that we met face-to-face. Her wild black hair seemed to have a life of its own, judging by the way it was standing on end. Her black eyes were snapping. Her mouth was curled into a bright red snarl. I don't know how she kept her lipstick fresh when she seemed to be in the middle of an emotional crisis, but fresh it was.

Anya shook her fists in the air. "You witch! What did you do to Beau!"

I had the sense not to answer, and she kept yelling.

"You trapped him somehow! Beau never had an intention of hurting you! And you nearly killed him! And you've accused him of killing his own aunt! How could you do this?"

I was still standing there, not answering.

So she screamed again. "Why don't you say anything? What do you have against Beau? How could you entrap him like this?" She took a step toward me and spoke again. "Are you crazy?"

Replying to this tirade didn't seem wise. I continued to stand there, staring back at her silently.

So she yelled again. "Why don't you answer me?"

I realized that replying to her was the stupidest thing I could do. But I did it.

I kept my voice low. "Where did you dig up Andrew?" I asked.

Anya's head whipped back. Then she took a step back. And she answered me, her voice quiet at last. "Andrew is my only friend," she said. "The only one I have in the world."

For a moment I almost felt sorry for her. Then her words chilled me. I wasn't sure why.

But I wasn't sorry to see her rush out of the shop. In fact, when I sat down at my desk I discovered that I was shaking.

Why? Why had the brief confrontation left me—I admit it—frightened? What exactly had happened?

First, as I had expected, Anya had started by berating me over Beau.

Beau had been inside my business at a time when he had no reason for being there, and then he had chased me around the shop with his face masked. *Duh!* Why would that upset anybody enough to fight back?

Thinking about how stupid Anya was made me feel a bit better.

And Anya had continued her dumb act. I refused to reply, and she grew angrier and angrier. When I finally did answer her, I didn't complain about Beau. I asked a question about Andrew.

And Anya's whole demeanor changed. She quietly stood up for Andrew. No yelling, no dramatic scene like the ones she usually performed.

Then she had fled.

What did her behavior mean?

She had dropped the drama when I asked about Andrew.

I had caught her unaware. And when I asked a question she wasn't prepared to dramatize, she stood up for Andrew in a way she hadn't used to try to protect Beau.

So, Andrew was her primary concern. Not Beau.

I helped myself to my stash of Chocolate Malt truffles ("milk chocolate filling covered in milk chocolate and embellished with a dusting of malt cocoa"). I pulled out two of them. Indulge, I told myself.

That gave my brain a jolt, I guess, and I went into the workroom and called Aunt Nettie up to my office, asking her to sit down and talk with me. I described the scene with Anya and reported my deductions.

"Does that sound logical?" I asked.

"Yes, it does, Lee."

I shoved my copies of the papers from Harriet across the desk, and Aunt Nettie looked them over. When she looked up, her face was troubled.

"You've given these to Hogan, haven't you?"

I nodded. "He wasn't in his office, so I don't know when he'll get them. But after what I said to Anya—I may have said too much. If Andrew is a con artist of some type, and Anya is working with him, and the two of them know my connection to Hogan . . ."

"Oh dear, Lee! They may leave town!"

"That's what I became afraid of. But I thought I might be imagining it. But I can't reach Hogan. If you agree with me . . ."

"Oh yes! Here! Hand me your phone. Maybe Char will let me talk to Hogan."

But no such luck. As a matter of fact, Char told Aunt Nettie that Hogan was involved in what she called a "major operation."

"I can't call him," she said. "He told me not to bother him at all."

Aunt Nettie hung up, and the two of us sat and stared at each other.

"He may know more than we do," I said. "He may be going at the same thing from a different angle."

"That's possible."

"But we need more evidence."

I studied that question for a moment. Then I spoke again. "Dolly."

"What do you mean?"

"My guess is that Andrew has been paying court to Dolly."

"Dolly? Oh dear, Lee! Why do you think that?"

"Because Dolly is really nice, but she's not conventionally attractive. Joe and I were talking about her, and we concluded that while Dolly would always have plenty of women friends, she was unlikely to attract a man who was worthy of her. This brought out a few remarks on the unfairness of life from me. Then I got a hint that Dolly had a suitor—the *Sports Illustrated* in her apartment the night she was attacked. I've never known Dolly to show any interest in sports. I hope it's not Andrew, but it could be."

Aunt Nettie looked concerned, and I went on. "There's only one objection to this theory. Andrew's goal seems to be swindling wealthy women. And Dolly doesn't have money."

"She does have some."

"Oh? She never acts like it."

"If Dolly had all the money in the world, she would live just the way she does now. That's how Dolly is. But last year she told me that if I ever decided that I'd like to retire, she'd like to buy into TenHuis Chocolade. She didn't talk as if she would be borrowing to finance it."

I could feel my jaw hit the office floor. "Why didn't you tell me about this?"

"Oh, Lee! Of course, everything I own will go to you. But if I outlive Hogan . . . And if I do retire . . ." She looked extremely distressed.

I jumped to my feet, went around the desk, and gave her a hug. "Listen, Aunt Nettie, whatever you do is fine with me. You just have to promise not to do any of it for at least twenty-five more years. You have to be around to run things."

She chuckled. "When I'm past ninety?"

"However old you get, we'll still need you to mix

that ganache. But don't do anything today. We've got other problems today. I need to talk to Dolly. Maybe I'll just ask her about Andrew."

If Andrew had gotten wind that Dolly had the money to buy a share in TenHuis, he well might have seen her as possible prey.

"That settles it," I said. "I've got to talk to Dolly, and it needs to be done face-to-face. Do you know where she is?"

"Oh, didn't you know? Dolly came home this morning. She's upstairs in her apartment."

Chapter 25

"What are we waiting for? We've got to talk to her!"
Before Aunt Nettie could reply, almost as if answering a cue, the street door opened, and Mike Westerly walked in.

His huge frame—all six feet four inches of him—automatically took over our little shop. Two of his giant steps brought him across the room. When he stood in the office doorway, he filled it up.

"Ms. Woodyard?" he said. "Is it true that Dolly came home?"

"That's what my aunt says," I said.

"Can she have visitors?"

"I hope so, because I need to talk to her."

Mike's face fell. "Oh. Then I'll try to see her later."

"Mike, my business is rather important. Give me your phone number, and perhaps she can call you when she feels up to another visitor."

Mike looked a little more cheerful at that suggestion. "Okay. And maybe I can go get her a few flowers anyway."

He wrote his cell phone number on my desk pad, strode out of TenHuis, climbed into his enormous pickup, and drove away.

Aunt Nettie stood up and turned to watch him go. "My goodness, he's a big fellow," she said.

"He sure is. Shall we go upstairs?"

"I can't," Aunt Nettie said. "I've got a sales rep coming in."

"What! But this is important," I said. "Can't that wait?"

"I just saw him drive past," she said. "He'll be in as soon as he parks his car. For three days I've been waiting to pounce on him."

"What's wrong?"

"I've got an earful ready for him. Their shipping department is really incompetent. I'm going to tell him I can always switch to another supplier."

"Do you need me to back you up?"

"No, I can handle this pip-squeak by myself. You go upstairs."

I got as far as the front door before Bunny ran out of the workroom and caught up with me. "Lee! Lee! I need to talk to you!"

Rats! Bunny was probably still trying to protect Beau. When I looked back at her I saw that her face was screwed up, I assumed in misery. I couldn't turn my back on her.

I went back to my office. "Okay, Bunny! I can talk a minute."

She was in my visitor's chair before I noticed she was wearing her ski jacket. She sighed before she spoke. "I haven't been to work yet today. Lee, Beau is in the county jail. I went over to Dorinda to see him, and his story sounds crazy. What is going on?"

I told her. I tried to make my account of the fight Beau and I had in the chocolate workroom sensible. It wasn't easy.

"Honestly, Bunny, I don't know what Beau was up to. All I know is that this guy wearing all black, including a ski mask, was chasing me. He had some kind of a club . . ."

"The handle of a plumber's friend."

I stopped talking and stared at her. "The handle of a plumber's friend?"

"What else could Beau find? He was hiding in the restroom most of the time."

I rested my elbows on my desk and dropped my head into my hands. I called to the counter girl. "Janie! Please bring us a couple of caramel truffles."

I'm sure I had never before asked Janie to bring me a truffle. I always got mine from the throwaway bin in the back.

Janie looked mystified, but she came into the office with two caramel truffles. They are described in our literature as "a soft caramel ganache covered with either milk or dark chocolate shell and embellished with a contrasting swirl." They are delicious.

I took one and handed the other to Bunny. "Here," I said. "This is an emergency. A plumbing emergency, I guess."

We each bit into our truffle. I chewed and swallowed half of mine. Then I began to giggle. Then Bunny began to giggle. Then we guffawed. Then we howled.

This went on for about five minutes before we were able to stop.

Finally, while mopping my eyes, I spoke. "I guess

the real question, Bunny, is how could you fall for such an inept guy?"

"When you're as inept as I am myself, Lee, it's hard to see that people who pretend to be competent may not be competent at all."

"You're not inept, Bunny. No more of that talk. But does Beau think that—well, even if he didn't bring a weapon with him, and even if the only weapon he could find was ridiculous, he still apparently tried to harm me?"

"No, he doesn't see it. I called Abigail's lawyer and asked him to talk to Beau." She leaned forward earnestly. "But I'm pretty sure that Beau didn't kill Abigail."

"I'm beginning to think you're right. Today I found out some things about Anya and Andrew . . ." I broke off. Maybe I'd better not share Harriet's information. "I don't want to talk about this until I've had a chance to talk to Dolly. And to Hogan."

"Is that where you were going?"

"No, Hogan is incognito—I mean, he's incommunicado. Even Aunt Nettie can't find him. I'm trying to get some information from Dolly."

"Do you know where she is?"

"Apparently she's home from the hospital."

I paused. What was I doing? I simply hoped I wasn't endangering Dolly. Or Bunny, for that matter. But with Anya and Andrew on the loose, I wasn't sure what was going on.

"You head for your office," I said. "I'll go talk to Dolly. I should be right back."

I went out the front of the shop and turned toward Dolly's front door. I jumped when I saw a white van a lot like Andrew's drive by, but it kept going. I rang Dolly's bell.

As usual, the window over my head opened. Dolly's voice boomed. "Come on up!"

The next few minutes were devoted to hugging and good wishes. It surely was good to see Dolly.

"And you look great!" I said.

"I feel fine," she shouted. "I don't know why I had to stay so long! The past two days I just sat around and watched television!"

"I'm sure glad you're home now," I said. "Do you need someone to stay with you?"

"Nope! I've still got that Sis to cook. Everything's fine! Plenty of groceries! Don't need a thing!"

"Good. But do you feel up to answering some questions?"

"Sure!"

"How much have you remembered?"

"Hardly anything, Lee! I still don't remember anything about being attacked. But Hogan swears that's what happened!"

We sat side by side on the flowered couch, and I began to outline my research into the origins of Andrew and Anya.

Dolly's face grew impassive; an unusual expression for her. She said nothing.

I clutched the manila folder containing Andrew's pictures in my arms. "Does any of this story mean anything to you, Dolly?"

She didn't answer my question directly, but instead used her finger to tap on the file folder.

"And what is this?" she asked. "You wouldn't lug it along unless you had some reason!"

I didn't want to go on, but I forced myself.

"The woman I talked to in Arkansas, well—she'd done a little detective work herself. She found three other art shows, most of them in Missouri, where some guy with a similar name had entered. At each show he met a wealthy, single woman. And in each case, after the show was over and he had left town, he instigated a sort of romance. All rather secretive. And each ended when the woman agreed to invest with him or lend money to him. Once he had the money in his pocket . . ." I shrugged.

Dolly reached over and took the folder from my hand. She opened it and looked at the pictures and the identifications. Then she grinned her friendly grin. When she spoke, her voice was actually quiet.

"I guess I didn't have enough money to appeal to him," she said. "My grandmother only left me a few thousand."

A great sense of relief fell over me. "Am I glad to hear that," I said.

"Or maybe he was just leading up to asking for money!" she said. "All he got out of me was a door key!"

I blinked.

"We didn't have anything like a big romance!" Dolly yelled. "He used to bring me a bottle of wine! I'm sure he stole it from the wine shop's stock! I'd cook dinner! I like to cook for people!"

"Oh, Dolly!" I grabbed her hand.

"Anyway, one morning I missed my keys! I called, and Andrew said he'd walked off with them by mistake! But he asked if he could get a duplicate for the back door! Said it would be easier to walk down the alley to see me, instead of coming through the front! Even though those cats always yowled!"

Dolly gave me a level look. "You know, I just didn't like that idea somehow! Too sneaky! I mean, we were two single people! He didn't need to tiptoe around to see me!"

"Oh, Dolly! You are so intelligent!"

"Well, maybe I didn't just fall off a turnip truck! So I told him I wanted the keys returned that morning, and we'd talk about duplicates later! I guess he still managed to get them copied! And it caused us all a lot of trouble!"

"Did you tell Hogan about the keys?"

"Not right away! It was kind of embarrassing, you know?"

I nodded.

"Then, after I got better, Hogan told me he thought there was a link between Abigail Birdsong and me! I guess because we were both attacked at the same place and in the same way! So I told him about it then! But I had no evidence that Andrew had ever used the keys! And I didn't know that Andrew knew Abigail! I still don't!"

"I think there is a link. I talked to one of Abigail's close friends down in Illinois, and this woman was sure Abigail was having a big romance. So it sounds like the same pattern. Surely Hogan will be able to track down someone who saw them together."

"But what were Beau and Anya up to?"

"Maybe Andrew and Anya were coming to the parting of the ways. Or maybe Anya was trying for Abigail's money through Beau, and Andrew was trying for it through Abigail herself. Maybe Hogan can figure that out."

It was at this point that the door to the back stairs opened, and Andrew came into the room.

Chapter 26

I state that baldly because that was the way it happened. Andrew simply opened Dolly's back door
and walked in.

He didn't kick the door in and jump through with
blazing guns. He didn't break in the door or kick it
down. There was nothing dramatic about the scene.

In fact, neither Dolly nor I screamed or yelled or
made any commotion. We just stared at him.

"Oh," I said.

"Hi, Andrew!" Dolly said.

It took me a moment to realize he was holding a
pistol at his side. "Lucky me," he said. "I caught both
of you together. The two women I need to talk to."

Dolly shouted her usual shout. "I heard that you
came to see me in the hospital!"

"Yes," Andrew said. "I was trying to find out if you
had told anybody about inviting me up for coffee. But
they kept saying you couldn't remember, and at the

hospital somebody was with you all the time, so I gave up. Until you got home."

Dolly looked puzzled. "Did I invite you up that night?"

"You sure did, Dolly."

"I don't remember it! I don't remember anything that happened that evening! But I guess it makes sense! They were saying that somebody with access to those back stairs had killed Abigail Birdsong, and I was afraid you'd made a copy of the keys! That would give you access! But, you know, I thought I ought to be fair! I thought I'd give you a chance to deny it!"

I was still holding Dolly's hand, and at this point I began to feel pressure. Dolly was talking to Andrew calmly, but she was squeezing my hand. Was this a signal? If so, what the heck did it mean?

I saw a movement, and I caught on. Molly, the tall red-haired woman Dolly called Sis, was coming in from the bedroom, moving toward Andrew. Dolly had known she was there.

But what could an unarmed person do against Andrew and his pistol? I willed my face to become expressionless.

Then Molly moved her hand, and I saw that she was not unarmed. She also was holding a pistol. Were we going to have a shoot-out?

Andrew came farther into the apartment, turning toward Dolly and me.

"Why have you come, Andrew?" I asked. "Dolly is supposed to be resting and recuperating. Can I help you?"

"Yes, you can. I need to know what you did with that scarf."

"What scarf?"

"The checked one! Black and white. I've got to have it!"

I spoke slowly. "But I don't know anything about a checked scarf."

"Oh, I know that's a lie! Beau tried to get it."

"He didn't get it from me. I've never heard a word about any checked scarf." I lied. Beau had mentioned a scarf. But I had ignored him.

Andrew aimed his pistol carefully. "Okay. If I don't get the checked scarf—and I mean right now—Dolly gets it."

And that's when the bouquet of roses floated in the back door.

I thought I'd lost my mind. I nearly laughed. The whole thing was ridiculous. But the door to the landing had opened gently, and this huge bouquet of red roses came floating in. Then an enormous face appeared behind them.

It was Mike Westerly. He was peeking around the door.

Was he one of the good guys or one of the baddies?

Whatever he was, I realized, he was between Molly and Andrew. And if we were dividing up the good guys and the bad guys, then Andrew definitely was in the bad guy category. So maybe Mike was on the good side.

Everybody seemed to be paralyzed. Dolly and I were facing Andrew without moving. Andrew had his pistol pointed at Dolly. Mike had come in the door—carrying roses—but was standing still, staring at the back of Andrew's head. Behind him was Molly, pointing her own pistol at Andrew.

But if she shot him, the bullet might pass through Mike before it hit Andrew.

Crazy.

Somebody had to do something. So I decided it might as well be me.

I dropped Dolly's hand and jumped to my feet, yelling. "Shoot me!"

Andrew swung his arm, trying to change his aim from Dolly to me, I guess.

And Mike hit him in the back of the head with a huge cut glass vase. Glass and long-stemmed roses went all over the place.

When Molly yelled—"Police! Don't move!"—it was an anticlimax.

Dolly, Molly, Mike, and I all jumped for Andrew, but he lay perfectly still, saving himself the fate of being stomped flat by four large, tall—angry—people at once.

As Molly pulled out a radio and some handcuffs, I collapsed next to Dolly on the couch again.

"So your sister's a cop?"

"No. My sister's a housewife! That's why she's able to keep an eye on Mama!"

I gestured toward Molly. "Then who . . . ?"

"Oh, Sis here isn't my sister! She just dyed her hair that color so she'd look like we were related! She's a cop Hogan knew! He rang her in as a bodyguard!"

"Oh! So this was a trap to catch Andrew?"

"I don't know what Hogan had in mind! But I don't think that he expected Andrew just to walk in like that! I think they lost him within the past hour! Anyway, nobody thought he was in this vicinity!"

Mike came over and knelt—actually got down on both knees—at Dolly's side. "Are you okay, babe?"

"I'm fine, Mike! I sure was glad to see you come in that door! But I'm sorry about the vase! It looked like a nice one!"

"I'm sorry it got broken. But I'll get you another for your collection," Mike said.

He put his arm about Dolly and kissed her cheek. And it was just as romantic a moment as it should have been.

About that time more police began to descend on the apartment. It seemed that it had been carefully staked out to catch Andrew, should he approach Dolly. But as Dolly had suspected, Andrew eluded them, and everyone thought he was in a different area. I found out later that Jerry Cherry had seen Andrew going in the back door, but he'd been told to wait for backup.

Hogan was livid over the delay that let Andrew reach the second floor.

The whole thing hadn't exactly been a trap, Hogan said. "We'd never put Dolly in danger," he said. "But we lost him, somewhere, and we wanted to be prepared in case he showed up."

The policewoman in the bedroom, who was pretending to be Molly, was from the Michigan State Police.

"I'd noticed that she had a superficial resemblance to Dolly," Hogan said. "I thought if we dyed her hair red—well, she might be believable as Dolly's sister. So I asked if we could have her for bodyguard duty."

When "Molly" joined us in the living room, I took a good look at her. "Sorry," I said. "I've got to ask. Did you ever wear purple feathers in your hair?"

She laughed. "Actually I did come down here to a Mardi Gras party. The purple feathers were part of my outfit. But my hair wasn't this red then. I'm naturally a sort of strawberry blonde. I guess the feathers looked okay; my picture ran in the *Warner Pier Weekly*."

"That's a load off my mind," I said. "Now if I knew

why I thought there were cats in the Dumpster, I'd feel halfway sane."

"That's easy!" Dolly said. "Field mice have nested there the past two winters! The wine shop's Dumpster has an actual hole in the back, next to the wall! And yes, they attract cats! And they made noises when Andrew used to walk down the alley! Sorry, Lee! I fibbed about hearing them! I guess I was embarrassed!"

"I'll call the exterminator," I said.

Other so-called clues were also resolved over the next few days. One of the Michigan State Police officers had found a short piece of pipe in our gutter. After a lot of testing, the scientific crew decided it was "probably" the weapon that had been used to kill Abigail. Whatever was used to hit Dolly never was discovered. When they asked Andrew, he denied knowing anything about the attack on Dolly. He was still denying it when he went in the doors of the prison. Nobody bothered to argue with him.

The final mystery to me was the scarf. I had no idea what either Andrew or Beau was talking about when they mentioned it.

We solved it by having every employee of TenHuis Chocolade collect everything she owned from our cloakroom. They gathered up each coat, hat, glove, and, yes, scarf. When we got through, there were two old raincoats, some torn boots, and one flashy scarf left unclaimed.

The scarf was black and white, designed in enormous squares. I recognized it as one Anya had worn. And I finally remembered that when I had interrupted the attack on Dolly, the guy with the weapon had been wearing a black jacket with some sort of black and white design near the collar.

Hogan's theory is that Andrew grabbed the scarf to wear when he went to see Dolly. When I interrupted his attack on her, he ran down the alley, and used one of the keys he had copied to enter our back door. He was afraid I would recognize Anya's distinctive scarf, so he ditched the scarf in our cloakroom, then ran on to the wine shop or to his own apartment. Later he and Anya sent the inept Beau to retrieve the scarf.

The ironic part, of course, was that I didn't recognize the scarf—not as a scarf—and ignored their whole effort. The whole thing was a waste of time.

I'm happy to say that Chayslee moved back into her apartment—until spring. Then she took a job on the Upper Peninsula. We hear from her now and then. And we miss her.

Bunny raked in her inheritance from Abigail. She turned the estate over to a well-recommended investment banker, sold Abigail's giant house in Shorefront, and moved back into the small house where she had lived with Beau.

I think she arranged for Beau to have a small allowance. He moved to Holland and never shows up in Warner Pier.

And Bunny's paranoia disappeared. I'm convinced it was part of Anya and Andrew's effort to speed her divorce from Beau. Anya, by the way, tried to hit the road, but Hogan charged her as an accessory. She took a plea deal in the end.

Bunny's doing just fine as the computer expert for TenHuis Chocolade.

And Dolly was back on the job in time to see that TenHuis made the deadline for Stella Drumm's Easter bunnies.

Non-Chocolate Comfort Food

FAMILY FAVORITE POTATO SOUP

When I've used recipes from my own family, they've always proved popular with readers. This soup is delicious and flexible, though it does not contain chocolate.

> Potatoes
> Onions
> Carrots
> Celery (optional)
> Chicken broth or bouillon
> Butter
> Salt and pepper
> Evaporated, regular, or skim milk

> **Garnishes**
> Sharp cheese, grated
> Green onions, chopped
> Chopped ham or dried beef

Peel two medium-sized potatoes for each diner. Cut up onions, carrots, and celery. Put in heavy kettle and add chicken broth, not quite covering vegetables. Bring to a boil and simmer, uncovered, until vegetables are quite soft. Do not drain. Remove vegetables and broth from heat and mash with potato masher. I like to leave them a bit lumpy. Add lump of butter.

Add salt and pepper. Stir in milk (evaporated, regular, even skim—your choice), making soup a little thinner than you want, because it thickens as it sits. Reheat over low heat; do not allow to boil. Each person can sprinkle with grated sharp cheese, chopped green onions, and chopped ham or dried beef to suit his own taste. Serve with soda crackers.

Everything in this recipe is "to taste." Vary the amounts to suit the number of people eating and their particular preferences. Any ingredient can be omitted or increased.

Ready to find
your next great read?

Let us help.

Visit prh.com/nextread

Penguin
Random
House